Hold You Down

Dominique Thomas

Copyright 2014 by Dominique Thomas

Published by Shan Presents

www.shanpresents.com

This book is a work of fiction. Names, characters, places, and incidents either are the product of the author's imagination or are used fictitiously and are not to be construed as real. Any resemblance to actual persons, living or dead, business establishments, events, or locales or, is entirely coincidental.

Dedication

I dedicate this book to my kids. I'm blessed beyond measure and I thank God for you all every day.

Acknowledgments

I would first like to thank God. With him I am nothing and without his love I would be lost. Thank you for giving me the talent to write. Your love is truly everlasting.

I would like to thank my parents. Barbara and Eugene. You two have given me all that parents can give their child plus more. I thank you both for always being there for me and for showing me that I Have to have God in my life to be full. For that I owe you the world.

To my husband and kids. Thank you all for being so understanding. You all are the reason why I write. I want to be all that I can for you. I love each and every one of you with my whole heart.

To my siblings thank you. We are a big beautifully blended family and I am so thankful to have each and every one of you in my life.

To my second mom and dad: Gail and Aubrey Sr. I just want to say thank you. The way you two have taken me in and loved me is truly beautiful. You have always been there for me and Aubrey and we love you both so much. Thank you for your love and support.

I want to thank my sisters and brother that I was blessed with having in my life through Aubrey. I love you all so much and I am blessed to have you all in my life. Thank you.

To my cousins both Cox's and Thomas's thank you all for the support and love.

To my friends I want to say thank you. Your friendship means the world to me and I am so happy to have all of you in my life.

To my Shan, I just want to say thankyou. I don't think you know how happy you have truly made me. My dreams are coming true and it's all because of you. You are a strong, educated, beautiful black woman and you inspire me! I could never thank you enough. To my pen-sisters the ladies at Shan Presents I just want to say thank you. Y'all rock and is so talented. I am so proud of each and every one of you. We are truly a family. At the top is where we will be let them talk about that!

To the book clubs that I have joined that have welcomed me with open arms I say thank you. The ladies at Myss Shan and Fam, The Keys & No Lock Book Club and the Talking with T.C book club. I just say thank you. We truly do have to stick together and support one another. I appreciate you all.

Last but certainly not least to my fans Thank You. I have my Super supporters that I love so much and you all know who you are. I appreciate you and all that you do. I hope that this book is better than my first. Enjoy!

Glory be to God. You are my father and you have always been there for me Lord. I thank you for all that you have blessed me with. You deserve all the praise. I ask that you continue to guide me Lord on my path to becoming the writer that I am suppose to be.

I would like to thank my husband and children. You're the reason why I write. I want to make you proud. I love you all. Aubrey, Caleah, Dylan, Dominick and Khloe.

I would like to thank my parents. Barbara and Eugene. You two are always there for me and I thank God for you every chance I get. Thank you for teaching me how to be a parent and how to love and worship God.

To my siblings. I love each and every one of you. We

might disagree about things from time to time but we always get back on track. We are a big blended family and I love you all!!

I would like to thank my other mom Gail I love you so much mom.

Text **SHAN** to 22828 to stay up to date with new releases, sneak peeks, contest, and more….

Synopsis

After losing both of her parents tragically Sophie is forced to drop out of college and support her two younger sisters. By chance she meets Ameer. He's everything that she wants but doesn't need. Married to not only the streets but to a woman as well. Sophie's sees that Ameer is trouble from the start but she can't seem to stay away from him. Ameer slides into Sophie's life and changes things instantly. Some for the better and some for the worse. With an enemy determined to take Ameer and his family out trouble falls onto Sophie and the ones he loves. Ameer has a plan and good intentions but getting to the finish line is going to be a lot harder than he thought. All he wanted to do was hold Sophie down. Will he be able to have the new woman and new life or will he succumb to his old one?

We met for a reason; you're either a
blessing or a lesson.

Frank Ocean

Chapter One

Sophie

"I don't like it and I'm not wearing it," Drew said walking out of the room. "And I'm tired of living in this little ass apartment!" she yelled and then the front door slammed shut. Erin looked at me and shook her head.

"She's spoiled as hell. You need to check her ass, Sophie."

I sighed and looked down at the clothes I had just brought. I'd spent my whole check on clothes for my sisters and once again Drew wasn't pleased with what I had. I picked the clothes up and looked at them. Yes, they weren't the stuff she was used to, but they still looked good. Hell, I couldn't afford to get her Chanel gym shoes. I couldn't even afford to buy myself that type of shit.

I dropped the clothes down onto the bed and looked at Erin. She was one of the most mature 17 year olds I had ever met. She was also a carbon copy of our mother. Tall, curvy and beautiful not to mention, extremely smart. I was really proud of her. Drew was beautiful as well she just had issues. Hell we all did.

"Erin will be fine. She's just hurting. The funeral was a few months ago and she's still grieving."

"And we're not? What they fuck! I'm tired of her," Erin said and started to pick up the stuff I brought her.

"Watch your mouth, Erin, and things will get better in time."

Erin finished grabbing her things and looked at me. Her slanted eyes held the same pain that I felt every day. We were alone. Besides my best friend's family, but their generosity only ran so far without me feeling like a charity case. All of my friends I had in college, we're gone. All of my friends from high school; gone, too. I learned a hard lesson when my parents died and their money went with them. People would fuck with you when things were good, but when they got bad you were on your own.

"Things will get better. Go get ready for school and don't worry about Drew. I'll go find her." Erin nodded and walked out of my bedroom. I slipped on my Toms and grabbed the house keys. I didn't know for sure where Drew would go this time, so I would just have to check her hangout spots. She had run away three times already and I was getting used to her leaving, which wasn't a good thing, but it was the truth.

We had grown up in a gated community and went to private schools our whole life, but things were different now. My father's once lucrative shipping company went bankrupt. Cars started getting repossessed and then it was the houses. The comfortable lifestyle we had known slowly started to slip away from us. Drew went home early from school one day and walked in on something that would change our lives forever. Our father the man that had raised us up with more love then we could have ever imagined was lying in a pool of blood next to our mother with a note lying next to him.

It simply said that he was sorry and that we would be okay from their life insurance plan and to destroy the note once we found it. That however wasn't the case. They had also been late payments as well and in the end we were left with $30,000. Most of that went to the funerals and we were down to our last. I would never tell my sisters that, but I was beyond worried. I had to drop out of college and get a job at my best friend's father's jewelry store.

The checks were nothing compared to what my father used to deposit into my account, but I wasn't going to complain. Money was money and we were surviving. I kissed Erin on the cheek before walking out of the front door. I climbed into my Mercedes; one of the only things that my father had paid for with cash and I searched through the nearby neighborhoods.

We now lived in Southfield, which was an hour away from the home we shared with our parents. Erin and Drew now went to a public school. The apartment was only a two-bedroom, but it was the best I could do and it looked nice. Drew was just being difficult and trying to give me a hard time. If she didn't like the way we were living then she could get a job and help out with the bills, so that we could afford a three-bedroom apartment.

I rode slowly through the neighborhoods until I spotted Drew at a corner house. She was standing next to a tall light skinned man with long hair that was pulled into a ponytail. I parked in front of the house and got out of the car. It was three guys sitting on the porch looking rugged as hell. Everyone stopped what they were doing and looked at me as I walked over to Drew.

Drew was a lot smaller than Erin and me. Whereas we were curvy she was thin and short. Still a beauty, she just took after our father in the looks department. I grabbed her arm and she looked at me. Her pretty face changed to a frown real quick.

"Get your fucking hands off of me," she said snatching her arm back. I couldn't believe that she had gotten so disrespectful when all I had ever done was look out for her and love her. She was starting to really piss me off. I grabbed her arm again and twisted it.

"Drew, you have 5 seconds to get in the car."

Drew's lips turned up and she smiled. "Or what? You're not my momma. Fuck you and them cheap ass clothes you tried to buy me."

I twisted her arm harder and she tried to punch me in the face. Some of the guys on the porch started yelling and laughing, but I didn't see shit funny. I pushed her down onto the ground because she really wasn't a match for me and pushed my hair out of my face.

"Now, your ass got two minutes to get in the fucking car, Drew." I turned to walk away and she jumped onto my back. She started to pull my hair and I pulled her off of me. She stumbled back and the light skinned guy with the long hair picked her up. He looked at me and smiled showing me his bottom grill that was diamond encrusted. I rolled my eyes at him because regardless of what the situation was niggas would try to holler at you. I looked at Drew. I couldn't believe my baby sister had actually tried to fight me. What the hell was really going on?

"Drew, get your ass in the car now!" I yelled and walked towards my car. The light skinned guy let her go and she looked at me. Her long hair was all over her head and she had this deranged look in her eyes. Shit maybe she was high or something.

"You know what? Fuck you, Sophie! You think you so fucking perfect. Dad used to always say Sophie's going to college, Sophie's going to become a dentist. If only he could see you know. Working as a fucking sales girl and wearing cheap ass clothes. I'm through with y'all," she said and started to walk away.

"And who's going to take you in then, Drew? Some nigga? What you going to do when he gets tired of you!"

Drew stopped walking and turned around. "Don't worry about me and I won't worry about you. You can keep all that bullshit you bought me because I don't need it." She turned back around and walked off. The guys on the porch started to laugh and the light skinned guy looked at them. They stopped laughing instantly and looked down at their cellphones. He walked over to my car and put his hands in his pockets.

"She cops weed from my young boy, I'll make sure she straight ma. I won't let her be out here tricking." His words were sincere, but at the moment all I could think about was how my sister had just walked away from me. Like I was nothing to her. I wiped a few tears away and opened my car door.

"You saying that now, but I don't know you and I don't need you to do shit for me or my sister." I climbed into my car and pulled off.

****

"And she's still gone?" Janelle asked. Janelle was my God-sister. We had known each other our whole lives and her parents my Godparents were the only reason I had money in my pocket.

"I don't know," I said and looked around the jewelry store. I needed to focus on something other than Drew. I hadn't seen her in a week and I was starting to worry.

"Well does Erin know about a boyfriend that she could be staying with?"

I shook my head and continued to arrange the jewelry in the display case. The double doors swung open and I looked up. The same light skinned guy that sold weed to Drew walked in. He looked good, but not my type. He was wearing a white t-shirt with black jeans and white sneakers. His necklace hung to his stomach and was covered in diamonds and so was his watch. I had only been working at the jewelry store for a few months, but I could already spot the real stuff from the fake and his was definitely real.

He walked over to me and I could hear Janelle let out this dramatic ass sigh. She was so extra sometimes. I looked at her and rolled my eyes. She laughed and walked off headed towards the backroom. I looked back at the guy and he was standing in front of me with a cocky smirk on his face. His light brown eyes slowly slid up and down my body making me a little uncomfortable.

"What are you doing here?" I asked skipping the small talk. I mean did Drew tell him where I worked?

"Hi my name is Princeton and it's good to see you again, too. I was actually in the mall shopping and decided to stop in and see if my watch was ready. I didn't know you worked here. I been copping jewelry from Johnny for years," he replied. I walked over to my computer and he followed me. I pulled up the inventory and looked at him.

"What's your full name?" I asked with an attitude. I knew he hadn't done anything to me, but even knowing that he was selling weed to my little sister had me not liking him already.

"Princeton Wright and why you so mad? Your sis is good. I put her up at a hotel until I could find her a place. My boy owns some lofts, but none of them are empty right now."

I stopped typing.

"Why would you do that? She needs to be home with me and her sister. You getting her a room will only enable her behavior."

"So, you would choose for her to be out on the streets? So any nigga could rape and beat on her?"

I stood up and looked at him. He was completely out of line. He had no right to come up in here acting like he was Santa Clause or some shit when he was one of the reasons why my sister was so wild.

"Your shit isn't back yet and you need to leave."

"Oh, really?" he asked and stepped around the desk. Janelle walked out of the back room and looked at both of us. I could see worry in her almond shaped eyes.

"Is everything okay, Sophie?"

I ignored the body heat that was radiating off of Princeton and I walked away from him. I made myself a cup of coffee as Princeton watched me with a frown on his face. He went into his pockets and pulled out two cards.

"Look here are two VIP passes to see Kasam. He's like a brother to me and so y'all will be good. I don't want shit from you or your sister. I simply saw she needed help and so I helped her. A thank you would have been nice."

He slapped the passes down onto the counter and walked away. Janelle watched him exit through the doors before walking over to me. She picked the passes up and her face lit up like a Christmas tree.

"Listen, I don't know what's going on with you and that fine ass nigga, but you better get over it. He just gave us passes to see Kasam bitch!" Janelle yelled and she began to dance. She grabbed the counter and started to twerk when her father walked into the jewelry store.

"Janelle cut the bullshit and get to work," he said shaking his head. Janelle stood up straight and quickly walked away holding the tickets. She looked back at me and winked before turning the corner. Johnny was my Godfather and I knew that I could count on him. My mother's family was in Minnesota and my father's family didn't really mess with us like that because from the beginning they didn't like the fact that he was marrying what they considered a middle class black woman.

My father's family came from real money, but it was things you had to do to get it and marrying someone that they didn't approve of was one way to get cut out the will. They didn't even console us at the funeral. They said their goodbyes to my father and they left. Johnny on the other hand stepped up to the plate and took us in. He even helped me with the down payment for the apartment.

"So, how are things going? Have you talked to Drew?" Johnny asked as he walked up on me.

"No, but I know she'll pop up when things get unbearable. This is the fourth time she's left and it won't be the last," I said while looking at Johnny. He was wearing one of his usual black two-piece suits and looking like he was in his late thirties instead of 55. Johnny hugged me tight and rubbed my back in a circular motion.

"I'm going to find her a counselor this week," he said.

I pulled away from him and shook my head. We all needed counseling, but right now I couldn't afford that. Drew would have to wait and Johnny had already done way too much for us. I couldn't let him pay for one more thing.

"No, I can't afford to pay for counseling and I refuse to let you pay."

"But I insist," Johnny said and smiled.

"She said no, anyway momma is on the phone." Janelle said as she walked up to us. Johnny looked at her and narrowed his eyes.

"Did you email those people back about the Canton location?"

"Yes, I did anything else, Daddy?" Janelle asked with an attitude.

Johnny ignored her and looked at me. He kissed my cheek and rubbed my arm before walking away.

"You're like the daughter he wish he had," Janelle said in a low voice. Janelle had always talked about how Johnny favored me over her. I couldn't see how she felt that way. He was paying her car note on her Lexus truck. Had bought her a condo and was paying her way through fashion school. It seemed like he loved her to me.

"Stop imagining things and fix your face, Janelle. Your father only helps me because I'm his Goddaughter."

"If that's what you want to think then okay, but enough about him. These tickets are banging and I can't wait to go see Kasam," she whispered excitedly. She smiled wide and I couldn't help but to laugh. Her happiness was infectious.

Kasam was one of the biggest rappers in the game and was even doing movies now. He represented Detroit every chance he got. I was in no way shape or form interested in seeing him, but I knew Janelle would kill me if I didn't go with her.

"Okay, we can go, but I'm not staying out late. I need to try to work some extra hours so I can get Drew this counseling that she needs."

Janelle looked at me and she smiled.

"I swear we'll leave right after the concert."

I looked at her and gave her a "yeah right look" and she laughed. She knew that was a lie. The concert wasn't the problem, Janelle's partying was. Janelle had no problem doing whatever when it came to men and that was one of the reasons why I didn't party with her like that. I would drive my car so that if she got to tripping I could easily slip away and go home. I could use a night out, but nothing more.

Chapter Two

Ameer

"What I can't seem to understand is how I have three sons and only one visits me? Nobody has a problem buying cars, flashing money and living like they the fucking man. Yet they have a problem making a trip out of state to see the one person that made them who they are. Is that not some fucked up shit?" Pops asked. I nodded and he continued. "Because this shit is just beyond disrespectful at this point. I haven't seen Aamil and Kasam in months!" he yelled and the guard looked at him. Pops eyed the guard daring him to say something, but he never did. Pops looked back at me and he shook his head.

"Is it too much to ask your sons to come see you? I been locked up for 11 fucking years, Ameer. When I get out next year things are going to change."

I sat up in my seat and rubbed my head. I had just gotten it shaved the other day and I already needed to head back to my barber.

"You know how they are pops. Kasam is in Miami doing a show and Aamil is going through some things."

Pops nose flared and he looked at me. Even at 30, my father still scared the shit out of me. Hell for 52 he was a big nigga. 11 years' worth of prison time would do that to you.

"What is he going through? You keep telling me he has issues and the shit just isn't making any sense."

I sighed and looked at my pops. I could tell today was going to be one of those days because he was on one. I came to see him faithfully. He didn't have a reason to be pissed at me. He could miss me with that bullshit.

"I don't know just things. He back beefing with moms and he got other stuff going on."

"Like what, Ameer?" he asked again.

I took a deep breath and exhaled. Even in prison, I knew that if I popped off at the mouth he would fuck me up. I rubbed the bridge of my nose and pulled on my beard to calm my nerves.

"Things. Now, have you talked to uncle Hashim?"

Pops glared at me. "Yeah, I have and shit sounds like it's all over the place out there. It'll be handled, now how is your mother doing?"

I sat back and smiled at him. He didn't have to worry about seeing me anytime soon. He was pissing me the fuck off. I knew we couldn't talk about much, but for him to play me to the left like that had me heated.

"She's good she gets out in a few months. She refuses to see Aamil and that's why he's so mad."

Pops cocked his head to the side.

"So, he can go see her, but not come to see me? Yeah okay, Aamil will be fine. He's a grown ass man tell him to buck up. How is Kasam doing?"

I smiled thinking about my younger brother. He had did something that none of us could do. Went completely legit and I was proud as hell of him.

"He's good."

Pops nodded. "And Tatum and Ahmad?"

I thought about the woman that I used to love and I shook my head. Money changed people and Tatum had let it change her into a woman that I didn't know anymore.

"Ahmad's good and Tatum's the same. Clubbing and shopping. She doesn't do shit for Ahmad or me. I'm real close to putting her ass out."

Pops facial expression told it all. He didn't like me talking about divorce, but shit things were different. They didn't make women like my mother anymore and he had to realize that. Tatum was a selfish bitch that I couldn't wait to get rid of.

"I already know what you about to say and I agree with you. Marriage is sacred, but you need to be telling my wife that. She acts like she's 21 instead of 30. I can't do it anymore. I've been with her for 10 years, how much longer should I wait for her to get her shit right?"

Pops did something that he rarely did, he smiled.

"As long as it takes. If Tatum isn't doing her job then it's up to you as a husband to get her right. Don't ask her to do shit, demand it. You're the breadwinner, a supposed leader. Guide her, Ameer. Stop finding reasons to divorce her. I thought I instilled leadership qualities into you boys, but maybe I didn't. Alana is a good mother to you all and wife to me because I will only accept the best. Tatum is giving you whatever because she doesn't give a fuck about the marriage and you don't either."

I gritted my teeth and looked away. I could take advice from my pops all day, but it was some things that he would just never understand. Tatum and I had been having problems for years now. I was tired of begging her to do right. If she wanted to run around being wild as hell then she could. She just wasn't about to continue to do that shit wearing my last name and spending my money.

I wrapped up my visit with my dad and promised to come back in a month. That wasn't happening though because I would force Aamil to come even if I had to bring him my damn self. I climbed into the back of my truck and Luke looked at me. Luke's father was one of my pop's best's friends. He watched my pops' back and Luke was now watching my back. It just turned out that way. I rarely went anywhere without him. We had grown up together and he was one of the few people that I trusted with my life. He looked back at me and he chuckled.

"Did you ask him about putting Aamil in charge?" I shook my head because I had honestly forgot and Luke nodded. "If you're ready to go completely legit then you have to actually let the game go, Ameer. Your real estate company is developing property all over the states and you're doing well with the record company. Kasam is bringing in more money than he can spend and then you have that new girl artist that I know is going to do well. You can do this, Ameer."

I looked at Luke and I sighed. He was the only person that was with me leaving the family business. Mason, my pops connect and friend was against it and so was Tatum. My momma was even asking me to stay in it for a few more years. To them we're at the top and what could be better than that, but to me it wasn't enough. Shit a nigga like me always wanted more.

"I'll talk to him, Luke, I just need a little more time. I gotta make sure Aamil has his shit together; lately he's been off. Then there's mom and Tatum. Once I take care of everybody, I'll tell pops about my plans."

Luke looked at me and pressed his lips together. He turned around and slowly pulled off. I was happy that I had him in my corner, but no one not even him knew what it was like to have the damn weight of the world on your shoulders. I couldn't just leave the family business without setting things up for Aamil. Pops wouldn't go for that and Mason wouldn't either. I had to do the shit right or it wasn't no point in doing it at all.

****

The minute I touched down in my city I went to pick up my son Ahmad. He was with my aunt like always because Tatum was out living like a damn socialite.

"Please come in, Ameer," Aunt Saniyah said opening her front door. Our aunt was like our second mother. Even when my mom's was out, Aunt Saniyah would watch Ahmad and come over to my house. She loved kids and I felt bad because she would never be able to have any of her own.

I kissed her on the cheek and followed her through the large corridor. My home was big and my parent's spot was even bigger, but uncle Hashim was living good, too. Somehow he had managed to build a little castle out in Rochester Hills. It was heavily guarded and Ahmad loved it there.

I followed my aunt into the family room and spotted Ahmad sitting next to my uncle. They were watching the news and eating pizza. I cleared my throat and Ahmad looked up. He dropped his food and ran towards me. I picked him up and hugged him tight. He was the reason why I did what I did. I wanted him to go to college and really make something of himself. I put Ahmad down and sat down in the first seat I came across. Aunt Saniyah grabbed Ahmad's food and they left out to give my uncle and me some privacy.

Uncle Hashim was a lot like my dad, but he was six years younger than him. He had done an okay job in my pops' absence and I didn't know how he would feel having to step down next year. I guess we would cross that bridge when we got to it. I knew things would be cool though. My pops and his brother were close just like I was with mines.

"So, how is my brother?" Uncle Hashim asked still looking at the news.

"Good."

"Did you tell him about your little problem?"

I relaxed in my seat and sighed. Uncle Hashim may have taken my pops' spot as head of the family business, but we all knew who was really in charge. Nothing went down without me there. I kind of felt like uncle Hashim was waiting for me to fail. That was why I was getting so pissed with the

Floyd situation. Uncle Hashim was using it to make me look bad. The shit was dumb. I wanted Aamil to handle the situation so that pops could see that he was ready to be in charge, but he was taking his time and this shit needed to be over with like yesterday.

"I told him."

Uncle Hashim looked at me. "So, what did he say?"

"That it was handled."

Uncle Hashim started coughing. He was a big man like my pops, but he was starting to get skinny. I wondered if something was wrong with his health. I knew if it was, he wouldn't tell me. I'd have to pry the information out of aunt Saniyah.

"You alright?"

"Yeah, just not feeling well. If Shadid says it's handled then it will be. I'll put my men on him and we'll handle the problem."

I looked at his ass like he was stupid. I told him to do that shit months ago and he kept saying that he needed to check some things out. He was on that bullshit. Again, he didn't want to acknowledge the fact that I had taken charge. I only asked him for things out of respect. I didn't need his fucking permission to do shit. Whether he realized it or not, I was handling all of the things he should have been doing. Anytime I needed my brother to step in, it was just for me to fall back.

I stood up and looked at him. I was definitely ready to go. No matter how much I did, my uncle always downplayed it. Treated me like I was a child. I was tired of playing this damn game with him. He slowly stood up and I walked over to him.

"I know you got things in order Ameer and well I'm…proud of you." He patted my back and sat back down. I looked at him for a moment before walking away. Something was up with him, I just didn't know what it was, but I would sure as hell find out. I put Ahmad's things together and we left. I needed to sit down with my brother and see if he knew what was going on with my uncle.

After leaving my aunt's home, Luke picked up my nigga Princeton and we took Ahmad to his favorite place. The bounce house. I watched him jump and play as I sat with Princeton. Princeton and I had been friends since we were kids. Outside of my brothers, he was one of the realist niggas I had ever met. He ran his own spots and even had a few businesses up under his belt.

I took a sip of my soda and looked at him.

"So, what's been going on?"

Princeton was tall with a muscular build. His ass was obsessed with working out. He'd always been called a pretty boy because of his fair skin and long hair and so he did whatever he could to show people that he wasn't a soft nigga. He kept his hair braided and was covered in a million tattoos. He even had a cross tattooed under his left eye.

"Shit that nigga Floyd still gone. I sat outside of his house all week and nothing jumped off. I think their ass up and moved. It's like I'm getting mad as hell because we can't find the nigga, but it's all good. I know were going to get his ass. If we go down to Memphis, we would be on their turf. I mean we know his momma down there and his sister, but shit they got a million motherfuckas watching them."

I nodded and watched Ahmad play. This nigga Floyd was a fucking headache that I didn't need. I needed for Aamil to get to him before my pops did. I needed him to see that Aamil could hold this shit down without me. Without the help of him and my uncle. If we had to make a trip to Memphis for Aamil to get this nigga to come out of hiding then, we would.

"Cool we'll get the nigga. Let's set up a meeting for later. What's Tatum been up to?" I asked already knowing the answer.

Princeton laughed and shook his head.

"She back messing with Nina. I had Bucks on them and he said they spent the weekend at the MGM downtown."

I looked down at my phone and my jaw tensed. I considered going to Nina's house and fucking both of their asses up. The bitch couldn't fuck me, but she could eat out another bitch? Yeah, okay. I was cool with her fucking Nina when I was involved, but now she was doing the shit without me and that was about to stop. Shit, I didn't have any side pussy, so she couldn't either.

I sent off a text to Kasam telling him about my visit with pops and looked up at Princeton.

"Look, the next time she hangs with Nina have Bucks snatch that bitch up and bring her to me. That shit went from a fucking onetime thing to a relationship. Tatum's ass is tripping. Has she been to see Ahmad?"

Princeton looked at me and he laughed.

"Nigga, what you think?"

I shook my head and dialed her number. She sent the

call to voicemail and I smiled. I had something for her carpet munching eating ass. Ahmad ran over to us as I was putting my phone away and sat down. He was my twin. We shared the same caramel colored brown skin and hazel eyes. He was my mini me. My clone and I would fuck anyone up that fucked with him.

"Dad, I had so much fun. Did you see me jump over that damn wall?" he asked excitedly.

I popped him upside the head not giving a fuck that we were surrounded by a bunch of older white people and Princeton started laughing.

"Chill out, Ameer, we was cussing and shit at his age. Let him do him," Princeton said.

I shot Princeton a glare and shook my head.

"I don't give a fuck what we was doing. He's too young to be fucking cursing."

Princeton nodded holding in his smile and looked at Ahmad. He patted his shoulder and Ahmad smiled at him. He was Ahmad's Godfather and whenever they got together they would stick to each other like glue.

"It's cool, Ahmad, yo daddy just acting like a bitch right now."

I punched his arm hard as hell and we all started laughing. We spent a few more hours at the bounce house talking shit and watching Ahmad play. I enjoyed the time I spent with my son, but in the back of my head all I could think about was going upside of Tatum's fucking head when I saw her.

Chapter Three

Sophie

I woke up to someone yelling. I rubbed my eyes and slowly climbed out of bed. I walked into the living room and Erin was standing over Drew and calling her all types of bitches and hoes. I shook my head and looked at Drew. Her clothes were actually new and her long black hair had been freshly spiral curled, it was her black eye that didn't look too good. She had been gone for two weeks, which was much longer than the last time she ran away.

"Drew, what happened to your face? Did Princeton hit you?"

Drew looked at me and she frowned. She had put some weight on, but it looked good on her.

"No, you sound stupid. Princeton is like my brother, shit he would never hit me. This guy I met at the club hit me because I wouldn't have sex with him," she said nonchalantly and sat back on the couch. I looked at Erin and she laughed while shaking her head.

"Bitch, you need to get your fucking life together! We have been looking for you for two fucking weeks and you come back wearing Armani and shit like life is good."

Drew looked up at Erin.

"You mad?"

Erin smiled and stepped towards her. I grabbed Erin's arm knowing she would light Drew's ass up and Erin looked at me.

"Go get ready for you finals, Erin. I'll talk with Drew. Do you need money for the bus?"

Drew started laughing and Erin closed her eyes. I watched her count down from ten before opening them.

"No, I'm good. I pawned two of my watches and he gave me $2,500. I paid the rent for next month and I have $1,100 left."

My heart sunk into the pit of my stomach. I didn't want my baby sister paying the damn rent. Dad had given her two Cartier watches for her birthday and I knew that they were worth way more than $2,500 more like $15,000.

"Erin keep the tickets on them and I'll get them back."

"With what?" Drew asked.

Erin lunged at Drew and slapped her across the face. Drew pushed Erin into me and she jumped up from the couch.

"I didn't come here to get hit on. That's why I left Tommy. I swear I am starting to hate y'all bitches!" she yelled and walked out of the front door. She slammed it and kicked it twice. I fell down onto the couch and Erin sat next to me. She rested her head on my shoulder.

"Why did they have to die, Sophie? Why would he do this to us?" she asked in a shaky voice. I shrugged and held off my tears. I needed to be strong for her. I was only two years older, but because of the decisions that our dad made, I was now the parent. It was the only way I was able to keep them.

"Things will get better," I said barely believing it myself, but wanting to give her encouraging words.

"When?"

That was the million dollar question that I couldn't answer. I kissed the top of her head and looked at the wall in front of us. It had a family picture that we took two months before our dad fucked our lives up. We looked so happy. If only we would have known what was headed our way.

"I don't know, Erin, but I have to believe that things will get better. We can never give up hope."

Erin nodded. "That's something mom would have said. Something she probably told dad before he killed her."

I bit down onto my bottom lip and looked at the picture again. We were the picture perfect family and now we were a bad episode of Good Times. I had no clue where we even went from here.

****

"Leave your hair alone you look fine. I can't believe your body has gotten so thick. Shit I'm jealous," Janelle said as we walked through the concert hall in search of the tour bus. The night had finally come for us to go to the concert and Janelle was too hype. When Princeton said all access, he wasn't playing. The moment we came to the venue people had catered to us. We ignored the other groupies that were backstage because the men quickly forgot about them once they saw us and we enjoyed ourselves. Kasam had done his thing on the mic.

I was wearing a sleeveless black Givenchy dress from my old wardrobe that had me looking way too thick. I had put on a few pounds since my parents death and thankfully it went to the right places. I chose to rock my hair in its naturally curly state and it flowed down my back effortlessly. I had on Janelle's black Christian Louboutin pumps and was feeling so sexy. Janelle wore a peach and white silk jumper with my nude pumps. We were both looking cute as hell and we knew it.

Janelle flashed our passes to the big, bulky, security guard that stood outside of the biggest tour bus on the lot and he nodded. He moved to the side and opened the door for us. Weed smoke billowed out of the door as we walked up the steps. For some reason, I had become so nervous that my heart began to race. I didn't care what Kasam thought about me, but I knew Janelle wanted to mess with him and I hoped for her sake that he didn't like her because I just didn't have a good feeling about him. He had a bad rep when it came to women.

"Well then, what did the bitch say?" a deep voice asked

as we stepped onto the bus. It was only four guys standing around and a bunch of women. I counted them up and shook my head. It was fifteen women in total and I felt sick. I'm not a fucking groupie, but being around these women made me look like one.

Princeton spotted me and he smiled. He sat down his bottle of Remy and walked over to me. I caught the eyes of a man that looked so damn good I had to blink twice to make sure he was staring at me. Before I could make my way over to him, Princeton walked up on me. He had on a grey suit with a white shirt and a black tie. His long hair was gone and now cut low to his head. I bit down on my lip because he was looking good as hell, too, and I smiled at him.

"Thank you for the passes, Princeton. We really had fun."

Princeton licked his lips and pulled me into his arms. As I hugged him, the fine ass man with the beautiful hazel eyes walked over to us.

"What's up, Princeton, who is this?" his smooth, deep voice asked.

I pulled back to give Princeton and me a little distance and Princeton looked at me. Princeton gave me a once over and looked back at the man. He smiled and I could see that they were very close. The mystery guy was a lot taller than Princeton. He had flawless brown skin with a baldhead and a full beard. I mean damn he was fine as hell. His eyes slowly took me in and he licked his lips. Princeton grabbed my hand and pulled me back to his side.

"This is the jewelry store girl I told you about. My little homie Drew's big sister."

Princeton's introduction kind of me pissed me off because it reminded me that he was enabling Drew to do the ignorant shit she was doing. I pulled my hand away from his and held it out to fine man before me.

"I'm Sophie."

"And I'm his wife," this irritating voice said from behind me. I turned around and looked at the woman. She was beautiful, but she looked tired. Her eyes had bags under them and her hair was lifeless and limp. However what she lacked in looks she made up for with her clothes. She was covered in diamonds and had on a beautiful Herve Leger bandage dress. I looked at her wedding ring and knew it cost close to a million dollars. All I did was sell jewelry; I knew the expensive stuff from the fake.

I held out my hand to her and she laughed. She shook her head and touched the bottom of her dark blonde hair.

"Keep it moving bitch, he's taken," she said with a smile on her face.

"Bitch!" I yelled pissed at how she thought she could dismiss me. I stepped towards her and Princeton grabbed me by my arm.

"Hey, what the fuck is going on?" Kasam asked walking up on us. He was shirtless and covered in sweat. He had on jogging pants and I couldn't stop myself from staring at his muscular chest that was covered in tattoos. Both of his sleeves were done and so was his neck. He even had one on his cheek that I had never noticed in any of his pics. I guess facial tats was what they was about.

"I should go, I wasn't trying to cause any trouble. Janelle!" I called out.

Kasam looked down at me and he smiled. He had a baldhead; too, along with a full beard only his was a lot longer than the sexy married guy's was. Kasam was also so light skinned that I was sure that he was mixed with something. His eyes were also the same hazel color of the married guy's. Of course they had to be brothers.

"Janelle is wrapped up right now. Have a seat and chill out. I'm a go change so we can hit up my party," he winked at me and walked away.

I turned around and bumped right into Princeton; he smiled and chuckled.

"Tatum, about to go ma', you good. Find a seat and I'll get you a drink."

I nodded and walked away. I sat down in between two shapely beautiful dark skin twins and the married guy caught my attention again. He stood with the woman that Princeton said was Tatum, his wife, and he stared openly at me. I watched her curse him out and not once did he seem affected by it. She turned to me and he grabbed her hand. He whispered something in her ear and pulled her away.

My phone vibrated in my hand and I looked down at it. I smiled when I saw it was a text from Erin. I hadn't wanted to leave her, but she urged me to go out. She was at home working on a painting.

"Are you having fun Sophie?"

"Um no but Janelle is so I will pretend I am. Is Drew back?"

Her reply came back seconds later.

"Hell no but don't worry about her. She'll be back. You

deserve a break and please call me if you need me. Love you and thank you for all that you have done.

I responded. *"Love you too."* taken back by her kind words and closed out the text as Princeton walked over to me. He handed me a drink in a red plastic cup and walked away. I watched him talk to a guy that looked just like Kasam and the married guy. Only his eyes weren't hazel and he had a low cute fade with a beard, he was sexy, too.

Almost as if they could feel me staring at them, they looked my way. I looked down at my drink to avoid their stare and took a sip of it after praying it wasn't spiked with nothing. After listening to the twins talk about how much they wanted to have Kasam's baby, Janelle walked out of the back of the bus with the biggest smile on her face. She walked over to me and sat down onto my lap. I looked at her and could see that her lips were swollen. I hoped it was from kissing and not sucking.

"Don't be mad he's just so damn fine. He asked me to spend the night with him," she whispered, excitedly.

"He did what!" the twin to my left yelled. She stood up and her twin stood with her. She looked down at Janelle and before Janelle could reply, she slapped her across the face. I knocked Janelle off of my lap because I knew she had never been in a fight a day of her life. I pushed one twin and punched the other one in the face.

Princeton and they guy he was talking to, grabbed the twins and dragged them kicking and screaming off of the bus. The married nameless guy followed after them along with his wife that gave me a nasty glare as she walked past. Janelle sat up and looked at me; her eyes were watery, but I knew she wouldn't cry. At least not in front of everyone. Janelle rubbed her face as Kasam walked out of the back. He now had on a navy suit with a light blue shirt that was unbuttoned at the collar. He licked his lips when he looked at Janelle.

"You good ma?"

She smiled forgetting all about her slap to the face she'd just gotten and stood up. She walked over to Kasam and hugged him tightly. He looked at me and stopped smiling. The coldness in his eyes caught me completely off guard. I stopped watching them and looked down at my nails.

"I've known you for five minutes and already you've caused all kinds of havoc," the deep voice said. He sat down next to me and he smiled. His lips were full and looked so soft. I smiled at him and licked my lips.

"I know I should have stayed home."

He shook his head and frowned at me. His thick brows sunk in and his beautiful eyes looked at me intently. He rubbed a hand over his baldhead and I caught a glimpse of his Audemars Piguet diamond watch. It was so beautiful I nearly fell out of the seat. It was covered in diamonds. He smiled and I noticed a small cut in the corner of his mouth. It made him even sexier.

"I'm Ameer."

I smiled and held out my hand. He shook it as he looked into my eyes.

"I'm Sophie."

He nodded and let my hand go. The sudden loss of his touch made me sad. Ameer sat back and his scent lingered over to me. He smelled so good I bit down on my bottom lip.

"Princeton told me about you. Are you two kicking it?"

I smiled and shook my head.

"No, I don't date the customers. Just a rule I have."

Ameer licked his lips and his hand found my thigh.

"Well then, I'm good because baby I'm the boss. What you got up for tonight?" he asked continuing to rub on my thigh. My body relaxed and different emotions started to flow through me. I could feel the need to have him build inside of me. I had only been with two guys and they were both young like me. I could tell that Ameer was all man and that kind of scared me.

"I'm actually about to leave."

"What no! The party just getting started ma," Kasam said walking over to us. He was back to smiling and I was beginning to think he was bipolar or something.

"Yes, Sophie, lets party with them all night. The girls will be fine." Janelle chimed in sitting down next to me.

"You got a shorty?" Ameer asked.

I nodded and Janelle groaned.

"It's her sisters actually."

I watched Ameer exhale and I caught an attitude.

"Actually, it's none of your damn business. Janelle lets go," I said and stood up.

"Aye, bitch calm down."

Ameer stood up and glared at Kasam. Kasam set next to Janelle who was watching us with a worried look on her face and he shook his head.

"I mean just chill out ma. We them niggas you should want to fuck with. We could be chilling with any bitch that we wanted, but were chilling with y'all."

I laughed and shook my head. If he thought that was an apology then he really was a stupid motherfucker.

"Janelle, I'm ready to go."

Janelle looked up at me and Kasam whispered something in her ear. She giggled and Ameer grabbed my hand. I looked up at him and he smiled at me.

"My brother just fucking with beautiful. Kick back and chill with some real niggas for the night. I promise you, you won't regret it." The way his eyes pleaded with me to stay made it hard to say no. He pulled me to the front of the bus and pulled me down onto his lap. I tried to move and he wrapped his arm around my waist. I looked into Princeton's cold, narrowed eyes and I looked away. I had completely forgotten about him and what was worse was that I didn't even feel bad about it. I didn't owe him shit and just because he gave us passes didn't mean I was going to give him some.

Chapter Four

Janelle

I sat next to Kasam as he talked with one of his boys. Sophie was pissing me the fuck off. It was like every time we got around some niggas with some money, she pulled this shit. I wasn't thick like her with long curly ass natural hair. I had to do a lot of shit to keep a d-boy's attention. I loved Sophie with all that I had; I just couldn't understand why she acted so fucking stuck up. Even in high school she acted like she was too good for niggas. The football players would want for all of us to have a little fun and she would chicken out on me.

Kasam opened my legs and put his hand in between

them. I looked at him and shook my head. We was still on the bus surrounded by a bunch of people. I liked adventure, too, but damn this was pushing it. Kasam however wasn't having it. He slapped my thigh and glared at me.

"Stop fucking playing with me and let me make that pussy wet girl," he said loud as hell. His friend started laughing and I looked away. My eyes watered as I opened my legs wider for him to get better access to my goods. I hoped that Sophie wouldn't walk back here. Not now. I wouldn't be able to take that because she wouldn't understand. I knew from the start this nigga was crazy, but I just couldn't pass up fucking Kasam. My ego was on 1000 already knowing that he wanted me instead of Sophie. I was usually seconds best when it came to her.

Kasam's fingers started going to work inside of me and I moaned. Everybody kept talking like I wasn't getting finger banged and before I knew it I was coming. Kasam pulled his fingers out of me and turned to his boy. They whispered something to each other and he looked back at me.

"Go back there with him ma," Kasam said and wiped his fingers on his pants leg.

I looked at his boy and frowned. He was cute as hell,

but I wasn't a fucking runner. I mean I wasn't anymore. Shit I was trying to do better. I was trying to get married soon; I had to slow down on my wild ways.

"Hell no," I said through gritted teeth.

Kasam grabbed me by my hair and pulled it so tight that I winced out from the pain.

"Bitch, if you think you fucking me again tonight then you going. I like for my niggas to sample the pussy I get. If I'm fucking then, we all fucking. Got it?"

The deranged look he had in his eyes told me that if I said no it was a wrap on me. I nodded and he let my hair go. I stood up and walked to the back of the bus with his friend on my heel. He followed me into the room and pushed me down onto the bed. I turned around and looked up at him. Tears slipped from my eyes as he unbuckled his pants. He laughed and shook his head.

"Bitch, what you crying for? You wanted the Kasam experience and now you getting it. Get over here and suck this dick."

I sat up and he walked up on me. I pulled his small but thick penis into my mouth and he grabbed the back of my head. He pounded into me for the next five minutes before coming in my mouth. He walked out of the room without saying a word and I sat on the bed in silence. I wiped my eyes and tried to pull myself together and the door opened again.

Kasam's brother Aamil walked in and looked at me. His eyes were kind, but I could still see the lust he had in them for me.

"You good?" he asked taking his clothes off. I nodded and started to get naked. I watched him put on a condom as I held in my tears. I closed my eyes when he walked over to the bed and grabbed my thighs. "Turn that ass over ma," he said and licked his lips. I flipped over and he slid into me. It started out slow and I imagined that he was my boyfriend and that he loved me. That maybe we would get married and have some kids. The harder he fucked me the more my fantasy faded away.

Aamil fucked me in every hole that he could fit his big dick into and to make matters worse, he left me $2,000 on the bed like I was some whore. I laid on the bed tired and sore. I had never fucked so much in one night and I had a feeling Kasam was just getting started with me.

The moment I closed my eyes the door opened again.

"Don't get tired now. You wanted to fuck and so I'm

giving it to you," Kasam said stepping in. I sat up and rubbed my sore eyes. He looked at me and then my body. I had cleaned up and brushed my teeth, but I still felt dirty. Kasam sat on the edge of the bed and held out his hand. I took it and he pulled me onto his lap. I wrapped my arms around his neck and looked at him.

"Why do you want me to sleep with your friends?" I asked him wanting to know the answer.

Kasam looked at me and he smiled.

"Why not? Your pussy is tight ma, I wanted them to feel the pleasure that you gave me. I like a woman that thinks of others instead of herself."

I smiled and leaned towards him. He turned his face and I kissed him on the cheek.

"But check this out. Is your girl down?" he asked. I imagined Sophie fucking like I did today and I started laughing.

"Um no. Why you want to fuck her?"

Kasam shook his head and rubbed my ass. I could feel him getting hard beneath me.

"No, that bitch think she's the shit. I don't want to fuck her ass. I do want you to get me right before the club though."

He patted me on the ass and I stood up. I dropped to my knees and pulled out his thick penis. Kasam groaned when I put it into my mouth. "Right there ma. Keep sucking a nigga like this and you'll stay around," he said and ran his hands through my hair. I smiled on the inside. He needed me; I could hear it in his voice.

I licked the head and sucked him with all that I had because even if it was only for a minute, he was mines. I would do whatever I had to do to keep him coming back. Kasam didn't know it, but I was about to be his baby momma. I needed a nigga in my life and he would do.

Chapter Five

Ameer

My phone vibrated in my pocket for the fifth time tonight. Tatum ass was getting on my last fucking nerve. She was mad that I made her leave, but she left me no choice. Trying to act like she can stop me from fucking with someone when she was still fucking with Nina was crazy. That bitch had some nerve. The moment I saw Sophie I knew I had to have her. Tatum must have saw it, too, because she started acting jealous as hell. I told her to act like a fucking lady and I made her ass go home.

I watched Sophie as we pulled up to the club. I could tell that she was ready to go, but fuck that. She was sexy as hell and I wasn't going to let her leave that easily. I knew Princeton was a little salty about her choosing me, but I knew he would get over the shit. She didn't seem like she was feeling him anyway.

The bus came to a halt and everybody stood up. I continued to hold Sophie close to me on my lap. I needed to talk with her in private before the drinking began and my brothers got wild. I wanted to see if she was going to be a quick fuck or somebody that I could fuck with for a while. I watched Princeton and Aamil pass by me. Then Kasam walked by with Sophie's home girl and our cousin Jeremy that was also his DJ.

Sophie looked at me as the last person stepped off of the bus. I just couldn't get over how fucking beautiful she was. She was rocking her hair how them chicks on YouTube and shit do. Natural and it looked good on her. It was long as hell and to the middle of her back. She had this blemish free brown skin that was actually glowing and then her body. Got damn I almost had a heart attack when I saw how thick she was. I had to hurry up and get Tatum's bitch ass off the bus. I was going crazy not being able to talk to her.

Tatum wanting to claim me and shit once she saw another bitch looking at me was comical. I had grown to hate her fucking ass. She was only sweating me now because I had her on a $2,000 a week spending limit for not spending time with Ahmad. That was what really had her ass trying to act like my fucking wife again.

"Look, it's been interesting, but I gotta go. I'll go grab my brain dead ass friend and we're leaving," Sophie said looking me in the eyes.

I smiled and put my hands on her thick hips. I couldn't put into words how beautiful her body was. She was definitely a ten in every department.

"Just stay an hour and then I'll take both of y'all back to your car. I just want to kick it with you, but before we go in there I needed to apologize for how my wife treated you."

Sophie frowned and stood up. She pulled down her dress that was sticking to every curve she had and she folded her arms across her chest.

"Look, you seem really nice, but this isn't me. I don't date married men and I'm not about to start. I have way too much stuff on my plate right now. A man that's not even available doesn't fit on it."

I stood up and towered over her. It was something about her that I just couldn't get enough of. I was addicted already and I hadn't even seen what the pussy was like. I touched her cheek and she looked at me. She acted tough as hell, but I could see it was an act. Sophie was defensive because she was tired of being hurt. Shit, I wanted to do everything but hurt her.

"It's all good ma. I don't want shit from you. I just want to put a smile on that beautiful face of yours. What do I have to spend for that to happen?"

Sophie took a step back and her beautiful face scowled at me. She was pissed. Good I didn't want no trick.

"Nigga, I don't want nothing from you."

I smiled at her.

"Are you sure? I mean I see how your girl gets down. I didn't know if you was the same way or not."

Sophie took a deep breath and she exhaled.

"I'm not and I never will be. Can we go now?"

I pulled her body against mine and I looked down at her. She acted different, but only time would tell if she was a hoe or not.

"Just give me an hour and you can go. I'm a man of my word ma. I swear I'll have my driver take you back to your car."

Her brow arched as she looked at me cautiously, but

she nodded. I smiled happy to see her give in and I kissed her on the cheek. Her skin was soft and she smelled good as hell. I hadn't hit shit in a while and I was horny as fuck. I watched her step away from me and lick her lips. Yeah, she wanted a nigga. I looked at her as I smoothed out my tie.

"Come on ma lets go celebrate my baby brother going double platinum."

Sophie nodded and together we walked away. Inside of the club, the music was banging. My eyes found all of our guards that the untrained eye wouldn't see and we made our way to the VIP section. I spotted Luke and I nodded to him. Luke looked Sophie up and down and he grinned. Luke hated Tatum and was always happy when I was with another chick. I'm sure he was waiting for the day that I would divorce her ass. Little did everyone know, that day would be sooner than later.

I shook a couple of people hands that I knew as I guided Sophie to our seat. The minute we sat down, Sophie's girl whispered something in her ear and they stood up. They walked away laughing and I watched them go down to the dance floor. Kasam sat next to me as he puffed on his cigar. I could tell from the look in his eyes that he was on one.

"So, is she down too?" he asked looking at them dance. For some reason, I felt protective over Sophie. That feeling caught me off guard because I didn't even know her. I watched Sophie move them thick ass hips and I licked my lips. Kasam was into some shit that I didn't fuck with. I wasn't cool with my niggas sampling what I had.

"Not this one. Plus she don't get down like that, I can tell."

Kasam started laughing and pulled a red bone model looking chick onto his lap. Her breast were big as fuck and hanging out of the top of her dress. Kasam whispered something in her ear and looked over at me.

"She too fucking stuck-up, Ameer. You showed up with a fucking runner, stop acting like you the shit bitch," Kasam said angrily.

I shook my head and stood up. I looked down at my baby brother and laughed. His ass was always fucking angry. A nigga had access to anything that he wanted and yet he still wasn't satisfied. He used to be happy all the damn time and then one day he just changed, but he never talked about it, so we didn't either. I knew if he wanted to bring it up he would and shit so much time had passed now, would it even matter?

"Nigga, chill out. You just went double platinum. Celebrate and stop bitching. I'll be back." I walked away before he could reply and walked downstairs. Luke stayed close by, but he didn't get into my personal space. I walked up on Sophie as some lame looking nigga stood behind her grinding into her ass. I patted his shoulder and he looked back at me.

"Get on nigga," I said looking at him.

The nigga looked me up and down and started back dancing. He grabbed ahold of Sophie's hip and she frowned. I could see worry in her eyes. I hope it was for that nigga and not me.

"Nigga, I won't say it again."

"No, he won't," Luke said standing behind me. I smiled as the nigga's confidence wiped off of his face. I didn't need Luke, but shit, why not use him? The nigga was on payroll. Luke walked away to give me some space, but I knew he was still nearby. I grabbed Sophie's hand and spun her around. I pulled her back to my front and wrapped my arm around her waist. Her sweet scent washed over me. I pressed her against my dick and she started to slow grind on it.

"You really trying to piss a nigga off ma," I whispered

in her ear. Sophie grinded her ass onto my dick some more and started slow winding on it. I was hard as hell.

"How am I doing that, Ameer?" she asked. Just hearing my name coming out of her mouth had me ready to fuck her.

"By dancing with that lame nigga. You walked in with me, show some respect."

Sophie laughed and shrugged her shoulders. She bent down and started to bounce her ass on me. I grabbed her hip and pulled her back up. I turned her around and looked down into her eyes.

"Dancing like that is going get you into some shit that I know you aint ready for. Don't play unless you ready ma." I grabbed her face and kissed her. Her hands went around my waist and I stuck my tongue in her mouth. Her lips were soft and her tongue tasted like watermelons. I pulled back to look down at her and suddenly we were pushed to the ground.

I reached for my gun as gunshots started going off. People started screaming and mayhem broke out around us. I looked down at Sophie and she was staring at me with fear in her eyes. Luke was fucking holding us down and shooting at the same time. The nigga was so big I couldn't fucking breathe and my damn heart was beating a fucking tattoo in my chest.

"Ma, we'll be good," I said to Sophie as she looked up at me. I hit Luke with my elbow to get him to stand up. "Luke, get the fuck up off of me! I gotta check on my brothers!" I yelled.

More gunshots fired and then a fucking Uzi started going off. Luke pulled me up and I grabbed Sophie. She tried to pull apart from me, but I wasn't having that shit. I picked her up and I carried her up out of the club. We climbed onto the bus that was parked right in front of the door and her girl was sitting on the floor in a daze with tears running down her face. I dropped Sophie off onto the chair and left right back off of the bus.

I followed Luke into the club as people ran out. The gunshots had died down and piles of people were hurt from either gunshot wounds or being trampled on. I spotted Aamil and Kasam in the VIP with Princeton. Aamil was holding his side while he leaned on Kasam. All of our guards was around and two of them were looking down at three dead guys holding uzi's. I ran over to Aamil and helped him stand up fully with Kasam on the other side of him.

With Luke and his men surrounding us, we walked out of the club and back onto the bus. I looked at Luke as Aamil slowly sat down.

"We're taking him to get some help. Get those video tapes."

Luke nodded and walked back off of the bus. I looked around for Sophie and her girl, but they both were gone. I wanted to go after her, but shit, where would I look and my brother was shot. My family would always come first. At least I knew she was okay. I could always look for her later. I rubbed my head and sat down as the bus pulled off.

"That bitch ass nigga!" Kasam yelled and threw his phone across the bus. "Fuck this tour and fuck this rapping shit. Put me back on and let me handle the nigga. He comes to our fucking city and acts like he the fucking man. Fuck what y'all been doing because the shit aint working and let me get at the nigga," he said angrily.

I closed my eyes and exhaled before looking at Kasam. I had just been fucking shot at I didn't feel like arguing with my brother. I knew his ass was hyped up and I needed for him to calm the fuck down.

"You know what pops said. You don't deal, Kasam. You legit nigga, deal with it. We'll handle Floyd's bitch ass and we'll do it before momma comes home," I said in a calm tone.

Kasam chuckled as he looked at me.

"Nigga, y'all better. If my fucking momma comes home to an ambush I'm fucking some shit up and I don't give a fuck who behind me when I do it. I started this rap shit because y'all said we needed a front, but now y'all taking this shit too far. I put in just as much work as y'all niggas and I'm the one that can't do shit. I'm not a little fucking kid!" he yelled.

Princeton sat next to me and I looked over at him. His lip twitched and we started laughing. Kasam was always bitching about not being included in the family business. Shit I wish all I had to do was fucking rap, my life would be fucking stress free. All this nigga gotta worry about is what to wear on a fucking awards show. I mean them rap niggas acted like they were in that life, but that was just an act. I knew all the niggas that was getting it and it sure as hell wasn't them.

"The shit aint funny you ugly motherfuckas!" Kasam yelled trying his best to hold in his own laugh. He sat down on the other side of me and I looked at him. Floyd was still hiding out like a bitch while taking shots at us. His ass needed to be got like yesterday. I knew that my dad said he would handle it, but I needed for Aamil to get him and now his ass had gotten shot. I was going to have to do the shit myself.

"Let's set up a meeting with everybody and come up with a way to get this nigga. The shit that happened tonight won't happen again. If he thinks the shit is a game then we'll show him that no matter what we always fucking win. Princeton go to his side bitch house and follow her ass until she gives something up. If after two weeks she stays away from him then, snatch her ass up and take her to that warehouse in Highland Park."

Princeton nodded and Aamil looked at me. I could see his ass was already thinking of a plan. That was all he did was plot even after being shot he was thinking about everything except himself.

"I'm putting together some shit, Ameer. I'll tell you about it later," he said and closed his eyes while clutching his side.

I looked at Aamil for a while and then looked away. Kasam made eye contact with me and I knew what he was thinking. If Floyd would have killed Aamil just how crazy shit would have gotten. Luckily for him he didn't, but that didn't matter. To us he was dead already and it was only a matter of time before we caught up with hm.

****

I walked into my house tired as hell. Aamil was taken care of and Kasam was staying with him at his house. I just wanted a hot shower and my bed. Luke went into his bedroom that was by the front door and I headed up the stairs. I looked in on Ahmad and he was asleep hanging off the side of his bed.

I fixed him so that he wouldn't fall and walked out of the room. I walked into my bedroom when Tatum looked up at me. Her eyes were wide as hell like she had been caught doing something. I frowned at her when I heard soft moans. I looked at my flat screen that sat at the foot of the bed on the stand and shook my head. She was watching girl on girl porn with a vibrator on her pussy. I laughed at her pathetic ass and started taking my clothes off.

When we met, we were so into each other. She came from a middle class family, but the minute I slipped inside of her, her life was made better instantly. I bought her a new car, a new crib, and gave her a bank account. Then we had my son and she started acting like a hoe. Hanging out all night with her ratchet ass friends and flossing on niggas with my shit.

The minute I caught her creeping with that bitch Nina,

I knew the Tatum I married was gone. She brought Nina into our bed and the bitch never left. Nina was a bad bitch, but she was just sneaky as hell and she had found a way to change my girl into some freak ass hoe.

"So, did you fuck her?"

I smiled and shook my head. This bitch had no right to care about who I was fucking.

"Just change those fucking sheets, so I can lay down. Matter of fact go to your room. Why are you in my shit in the first place?"

Tatum frowned and sat up on her knees in the bed. Even with her flaws, she was still bad as hell. She had golden brown skin with long dark blonde hair that was all hers. Perky small breast and a soft round ass. I looked her and up and down and I thought about fucking her. Shit I wished I could be sliding up in Sophie, but that would have to wait.

"I'm straight on you, but change these fucking sheets, Tatum."

Tatum stood up and walked over to me.

"Stop acting like a pussy and come fuck me or do that bitch got you whipped already? I mean she was bad as hell. We could share her, but you aint going nowhere nigga so don't get any ideas."

I grabbed Tatum by hair and made her look up at me. She liked it rough. She smiled wide and licked her lips. I let go of her hair and I picked her up. I carried her over to the bed and dropped her onto that bitch. She flipped onto all fours and I grabbed a condom from my top drawer. Tatum already neglected Ahmad. It was no way in hell I was going to get her pregnant again. Fuck that.

Once the condom was on, I grabbed a chunk of her hair and she moaned. I pulled that shit tight as hell and I slammed into her. Tatum began to throw it back at me and I fucked her until she came hard as hell onto my dick. I came minutes later and pulled out of her. I slapped her ass and watched it jiggle.

"Change these sheets and go to your room. I want to sleep alone."

Tatum rolled onto her back and she looked up at me. For the first time in a longtime, she actually looked hurt. The shit shocked the hell out of me, but I didn't let it change my decision.

"Just do it, Tatum."

She nodded and wiped a tear from her eye.

"So, do you even still want me?"

I looked at her sad eyes and wanted to make her feel better, but she had been fucking up for far too long and I just couldn't get over all the shit she had done.

"I do for now, Tatum. Change my shit and go." I walked away before she could reply and went to my bathroom to take a shower.

Chapter Six

Tatum

I woke up alone and angry as hell. Ameer was a fucking bitch. I was the mother of his kid and his wife and he played me like I was some side bitch. I had something for his ass though. I watched him cheat on me for years and the moment I bring someone home, I was the bad guy. He was just mad that Nina ate me better than he ever could. Nina was a bad bitch, but at the end of the day that was what was also holding her back.

The strap-on's just wasn't for me. I needed something hard inside of me and Ameer was it, but he had been acting salty as hell to me for the last few years. He made me sleeping in one of the guest rooms and even put me on a fucking $2,000 allowance like I was his fucking child. I mean $2,000 really? That's not even a fucking complete outfit and he thought that shit would be okay.

I shook my head at his childish ass ways and climbed out of the bed. Ahmad walked into the room and I groaned. Here we go. His little ass was always in my damn face. He walked over to me and hugged my leg.

"Momma, lets go to the bounce house today!"

Bounce house, bounce house. That's all I heard every time I watched him. Ameer's fucking brothers had spoiled his little ass rotten. I didn't go shopping every day and I deserved to, so what made him think he could play all damn day? Life wasn't fair and he needed to learn that now.

"Momma has to handle some business today. Luke is taking you to your Auntie Saniyah's house."

Ahmad pouted and I pushed his arm. He looked up at me with them same damn hazel eyes that his father had. Eyes that now held hate and disgust for me and I pushed him again. For some reason, I wanted him to hurt. It was like the more Ameer hurt me the more I hated Ahmad.

"Fix your face and go put on some damn clothes.

You're way too spoiled, Ahmad. That shit stops now."

Ahmad's shoulders slumped and he walked away. His head was hung low and I could tell he was hurt. As soon as he walked out of the room and closed the door, I smiled. Ha, ha. That's what his little ass get. Maybe next time he'd think twice before coming in here and waking me up. He had a nanny shit, get on her fucking nerves not mines. I carried him for nine months I put my time in. I wasn't on the clock anymore, but that bitch was.

I grabbed my hookah from off of my dresser and walked back over to the bed. I sat down and the bedroom door opened back up. Ameer walked in looking good as hell in a cream two-piece suit with a black shirt. He ran his head over his baldhead and looked at me. My pussy was good and wet for him and he hadn't even touched it yet.

"Get your lazy ass up and take your fucking son to the damn bounce house. Stay out of the city and always ride with Reem. It's some shit going on and I don't have time to worry about you. Okay?" he said with an attitude.

Well damn hi to you, too. I took a few pulls off the hookah and blew the smoke out of my nose. Fuck him, his son, and his rules.

"Yeah, yeah, I know. Good morning to you too dear husband."

Ameer closed the door behind himself and walked over to me. He grabbed my face and forced me to look up at him. I liked it rough. I smiled and he tightened the grip.

"Bitch, I'm not fucking playing with you. Stay out of the city and get up off of your ass. I don't really give a fuck about what happens to you, but if my son gets harmed because of your stupidity, you will wish you were dead. Do you hear me, Tatum?"

I nodded as my heartbeat sped up. His ass wasn't playing today. Ameer looked at me for a moment before letting my face go. He walked away and the door slammed shut behind him. I threw the hookah onto the floor and fell back on the bed. This nigga just didn't give a flying fuck about me anymore and that shit hurt me to the core.

Okay so I wasn't the perfect momma, but tell me who was? I loved Ahmad I just didn't need him up under me all of the damn time. I was still in love with Ameer he just didn't love me anymore and instead of being a man and saying it, he was putting it all on me. We were pre-nup free. I wish he would leave me, hustler or not, his ass was going to be paying me a lovely amount of money on a monthly basis and he could keep the kid. If I didn't have the man then, I had no need for the child.

****

Later on that day after leaving the bounce house, I had Reem take Ahmad and me to Nina's place. Like the good old boy he was he did it and sat his fine ass outside instead of going home. I sent Ahmad upstairs for a nap or to do whatever, so Nina and I could smoke and talk. Nina stayed not too far from me in Northville in a nice sized condo.

She didn't have a man or a job, but she had money. Her parents left her a trust fund and every guy that she dealt with always left her with some stacks. The bitch slept to 3pm, shopped whenever she wanted, and loved to party. She was my kind of girl.

"So, tell me why you got that mean ass nigga sitting outside of my house?" Nina asked as she broke down the blunt. Nina was beautiful. She was Korean and black and she never had a problem getting a man. Her hair was long and almost touched her ass and she had a body to die for. She had paid over $30,000 for her breast implants and butt injections alone. She was super thick like that bitch that Ameer was staring at the night of Kasam's concert. I took off my Chanel sneakers and kicked my feet up on her marble table.

"Because Ameer is acting like a bitch and putting me on lockdown. Something must be going down because he forbade me from going to the city."

Nina looked at me and she started laughing. She laughed so hard that her big brown eyes started to water. She ran her long stiletto nails through her inky black hair and she shook her head.

"Bitch, are you 30 or 13? I wish a nigga would tell me where the fuck I can and can't go. He foul as hell for that one and look at you following his fucking orders like a good little bitch."

I rolled my eyes and ignored her. She was always talking that hating shit because she couldn't find anyone to love her ass. She was too fucking shady and the niggas just didn't trust her anymore. They would fuck her and leave her alone.

"Bitch, get that hating out of your system. At least I could find a nigga to love and marry me."

Nina laughed. "And how is that working out for you? The nigga barely fucks you and treats you like you're his fucking kid. If that's marriage then I'm straight on that shit anyway," she said.

My cellphone started ringing and Floyd's name popped up onto the screen. He had been trying to get me to set up Ameer for a while now. Unbeknownst to Ameer and his family, Floyd was my brother's best friend before he died. We use to mess around, but once I met Ameer all of that stopped. Floyd got insanely jealous and decided to come up north and take over Ameer and his family's spots.

Floyd was that nigga, but even he wasn't a match for Ameer. The Matin family was living legends and had more money than they knew what to do with. I would be dumb as hell to side with Floyd. His ass was lucky for now because he was hiding out, but once they found him his reign would come to an end and make no mistake they were going to find him.

Hell their father was still running shit and he had been in prison for a thousand damn years. Nigga better than me because I would have been snitched. I was too sexy to do time.

"So, what you going to do about your boy" Nina asked lighting the blunt.

I shrugged and declined another blocked call from

Floyd.

"Nothing, I'm not helping him do shit. Ameer might not fuck with me like he used to, but he is still my husband and he loves me. Floyd's ass is playing a dangerous game."

Nina nodded and took a pull off the blunt. She held it in for as long as she could and then blew the smoke out of her mouth.

"And when that nigga decides to leave you?"

I grabbed the blunt from her and smiled.

"Then I'll hand his ass over to Floyd on a fucking diamond encrusted platter."

Nina laughed and I took a hit off the blunt. Ameer could leave me if he wanted to and it would be the worst mistake of his life.

Chapter Seven

Sophie

Two weeks had passed since the club shooting and I was still numb. I could have died and my sisters would have been alone in this world. The weight of that had me feeling all kinds of fucked up. I just wished that day would have never happened. Johnny gave me some paid time off and I had been spending all of my time with Erin. Drew was still gone. She would text us every couple of days and say that she was alive. Honestly, I didn't know what to do with her.

It took all of the savings that I had, but I was able to put

Erin back in her art school and she had been so happy. Her smile and happiness made it worth it. I'd also paid $300 for counseling that Drew didn't even show up to. When my parents were alive, she was the perfect child or so I thought. I was now starting to think that Drew had always been like this and that maybe I was just too caught up with my own life to pay any attention to hers. I was a full time college student and I had just dealt with a bad relationship when my dad killed my mom and himself.

My thoughts drifted to Ameer when Erin and Janelle walked into the bedroom and plopped down onto my bed. Janelle had been kicking it with Kasam and was claiming that they were in love. I loved her, but even I couldn't believe that shit. Janelle fell in love with every guy that she slept with. She was better than me though because I didn't plan on seeing those niggas ever again.

My phone started to ring and I saw it was my ex Marcus calling me and I declined the call. He hadn't called me in months, what the hell did he want after all this time? I quickly blocked his number on my phone wondering why I hadn't done that in the first place.

"Ameer?" Janelle asked sitting down onto the bed. I

looked at her and I frowned.

"Ameer doesn't have my number."

Janelle smiled and started giggling. Erin looked at her and she rolled her eyes. Erin had always disliked Janelle. I never really knew why.

"So, Erin was telling me that she was taking those art lessons again. I didn't know Johnny was paying you that much," Janelle joked.

Erin groaned and Janelle and I looked at her. I narrowed my eyes warning her to be nice and she smiled.

"What?" she asked innocently. I shook my head and looked back at Janelle. I hadn't seen her in a few days and I could tell she was up to something.

"So, what's up?"

Janelle gave me a big smile and smoothed out the wrinkles in her pants. Today she looked really cute in black slacks with a tan silk top that had a plunging neckline.

"Daddy said he's giving you another week to take off. After the accident, he treats you like your glass."

"Accident?" Erin asked with an attitude. Janelle could say stupid stuff, but she meant no harm. She thought that calling my parent's tragic death an accident was a nice way to put it. Erin disagreed.

"Erin," I said in a stern voice and she turned around. She sat at the edge of my bed and pulled her cellphone out. I looked back at Janelle and she had a confused look on her face.

"Um, okay, but yeah, like I was saying after that stuff happened something in him changed. He pampers you all of the time, Sophie. He also deposited your check into your account early. I heard him telling momma that he's going to pay your tuition for school. Shit he's going all out for you."

Erin sighed dramatically at the foot of the bed. Something had to be wrong because she had never been this irritated with Janelle before.

"He just loves me and more so he feels bad about what happened. I'm not going to accept any more things from him though. I just can't."

Janelle nodded while looking at me and I could hear a deep voice coming from out of the living room. I jumped out and ran out into the living room. Sitting on my couch with a Mexican guy was Ameer across from him was Drew. I smoothed back my hair that was in a messy bun and I exhaled. Two of my biggest problems were sitting right across from each other in the living room. Drew's black eye was gone and she was dressed like she was 16 again. I wanted to say that she looked normal, but hell what was that?

I turned to Ameer and put my hands on my hips. He looked good, hell he looked really good and that pissed me off even more. His clothes were simple a white V-neck with some blue jeans and some Jimmy Choo fish scale sneakers. It was the way his muscular arms looked in the shirt that had me licking my lips. I noticed his full sleeves and then I spotted his Cartier watch and his Cartier necklace that matched it. When I finally looked at him, he had this slick ass grin on his face.

"The only experience I had with you ended in gunfire. You need to leave and don't come back," I said looking at Ameer.

"Oh, this sounds interesting. I didn't know you was creeping with Ameer, Sophie. You done came up," Drew said and licked her lips. I looked at her and I said a quick prayer to God asking him to shut her mouth. I didn't want to fight her not right now in front of Ameer; that would be so embarrassing.

"Drew, come in the back we need to talk," Erin said walking up next to me. I watched Ameer look at her and then

Drew. He didn't look at them in a lustful manner and I was glad. I wasn't having that shit. Drew slowly stood up and she followed Erin to the back of the apartment. Janelle walked towards us and she gave me a small smile. It was clear who gave my address away.

"Don't be mad and I gotta go. Drew and Erin both scare me girl, I'll talk to you later." Janelle kissed me on the cheek and left. The Mexican guy followed her out and shut the door behind himself.

"I want to make it up to you, Sophie. I don't chase women and I don't beg, but you got me breaking all the rules ma. Get dressed, so you and your sisters can come with me," he said and stood up. I looked into his hazel eyes and I wanted to say yes, but I couldn't. He was obviously into some dangerous shit and I just couldn't risk losing me or my sisters.

"No, I can't. For one, you have a wife and secondly you have somebody after you. I mean you're walking around with a fucking bodyguard. Leave me alone and go home to your wife, Ameer." I managed to push his hands away and he looked at me.

"I wouldn't come near you if it wasn't safe. I'm not even cut like that ma. I just want to get to know you. I don't take no for an answer and so, I'll sit in here all damn day until you say yes."

He kissed my cheek and he sat back down on the loveseat. I watched him pull out his cellphone and I rolled my eyes.

"Ameer, you could be with any woman that you wanted including your wife. Why are you here trying to get with me? I'm not looking for a man and definitely not a married one. You need to leave before I call the cops."

Ameer stretched out and looked up at me. His full lips quirked up and he smiled.

"Call them, I'm sure they'll leave once they see who you got up in here with you."

I glared at him and we stared at each other for what seemed like forever. I turned away first and he started laughing. I walked out of the living room and into my bedroom. Erin was grinning like a Cheshire cat while Drew was playing a game on her cellphone.

"He's fine as hell, Sophie," Erin said and smiled.

Drew looked up at me and she nodded.

"He paid, too. Word is he a millionaire. I mean he's married, but so what? Obviously, the shit isn't working out if he's here."

I shook my head and closed the bedroom door. I looked at my sisters. They were both on their way to being gorgeous young women. I didn't want them to think that dating a married man was okay. Our life was already fucked up. I didn't know if I should bring Ameer into the equation, he could be the last thing we needed.

"Look he likes me and well to tell the truth, I like him too, but I won't do anything with him if y'all don't approve. It's not okay to date a married man not ever, but he obviously has marriage issues. He wants to take us out somewhere. I say we go to appease him and then after that I'll find a way to get him to stop liking me. I mean he has to accept the fact that I don't want him."

Drew rolled her eyes when she looked at me and Erin smiled. Erin arched her brow and ran her fingers through her long brown hair.

"He's really cute, Sophie. I mean maybe his marriage isn't what you think it is. They could be separated. I know you and I know you don't date married men. Hell, you've only had two boyfriends at 19. I've had like 3 and I'm 17. Ain't no telling how many boyfriends Drew has had."

"None of your damn business," Drew said looking back down at her phone.

"It'll be just a quick trip and then he's out of our lives forever," I said and looked at them. Drew looked at me and slipped her phone into her pocket.

"Sophie, no one tells Ameer no. He could be our ticket up out of here. Use him, hell men use women all of the time," she said and smiled at me. Erin looked at her and shook her head. They really and truly were like night and day.

"You just don't get it. It's not all about money. What the hell happened to you, Drew?" Erin asked.

Drew looked at both of us and for a moment I thought that she would confess her secrets. We all had them, but she didn't instead she looked at us and rolled her eyes.

"Well, let's see my parents died and I went from living a life worry free to being poor overnight. I can't see what could be wrong with me," she said and put her finger on her lip.

"Well, it didn't just happen to you," Erin shot back at her. Drew looked at her and nodded.

"No, it didn't, but I'm the only that's acting like it happened. You two keep pretending and I can't get with that

fake shit, but anyway let's go spend up some of Ameer's
money. I can't believe Sophie snagged the richest nigga in the
city's attention. Who knew you had it in you?"

I ignored Drew and changed into some skinny jeans.
After we were all ready, we walked back into the living room.
Ameer sat on the couch with my remote in his hand. He
looked at me and then at my sisters. He sat the remote down
and stood up.

"I'm Ameer, who are you beautiful ladies?" Erin
actually blushed when he looked down at her.

"That's Erin and Drew, my little sisters."

Ameer smiled and grabbed my hand. He pulled me to
his side and kissed me on the cheek.

"Wow, they're beautiful just like you, Sophie. Do y'all
like Air Time?" The girls nodded and he smiled. "My son
does. We're going to pick him up and go there, then we can go
get something to eat," he said and looked at Drew. His eyes
went to her crop top and he shook his head. "You going to
have to go change that shirt sis. I don't want to catch a case
not today anyway."

Drew frowned and looked at me. I smiled because he
was looking out for her and it was cute. He was telling her

something that she needed to hear. Ameer wrapped his arm around my waist and pulled me to his side. His intoxicating scent washed over me as he looked back at Drew.

"I'm only looking out for you. You gotta respect yourself if you want a nigga to respect you. Wearing shit like that will make them want you for sex and nothing else," he said.

"Well, my daddy is dead. You might run the streets, but you don't run shit up in here," Drew said and with an attitude. I could feel Ameer's body tense up next to me.

"Drew, watch your language and go change your top. Now," I told her.

Drew glared at me and then glared at Ameer. "Two seconds in and he already running shit around here," she mumbled walking out of the room. Ameer looked down at me with a small smile on his face.

"She always act like that?"

"Unfortunately," Erin replied. Aamil looked at her and he laughed.

"Well, I can go round for round with her ass. She just needs a good ass whopping. I whoop teenagers, too, I don't give a fuck."

Erin laughed and he joined in with her. This felt right and wrong at the same time. Ameer looked down at me and he licked his lips.

"I promise won't nothing happen to you or your sisters while you're with me," he said like he could sense my reluctance to leave with him. I nodded and grabbed my house keys and cellphone. Once Drew was changed into a longer shirt that covered her belly button, we left.

****

A few hours later, we sat inside of Air Time while the girls played with Ahmad. What was crazy was that the minute they saw him it was like he was a part of the family. He clung to both of them and they showered him with hugs and kisses. He was just adorable and so handsome. He had a slight cursing problem that I didn't want the girls to make worse. They already talked like sailors. He'd said hell a few times since we'd been here and he'd said shit.

Drew laughed, but Ameer didn't think it was funny and he told him to stop it, which was a good thing. I needed to be stricter with the girls; it just felt weird because I wasn't that much older than them and I was giving them rules. I was happy to see that Ameer didn't condone things like that.

"So, tell me your story, Sophie," Ameer said sitting down next to me. He handed me my drink and a slice of pizza. The girls and Ahmad had decided to eat here instead of Benihana's, which would have been our next stop.

I took a sip of my lemonade and looked at Ameer. This whole situation was crazy to me. I had to find a way to get rid of him because what he thought he wanted from me he really didn't. Not only was he a taken man, but I was broken woman. My ex-boyfriend left me with scars that would never heal.

"You tell me yours first starting with where your wife is," I said and took a bite of my pizza.

Ameer touched my cheek and then my neck. Just a simple touch had me on fire. His finger slid back up my neck and he outlined the shape of my lips with it. I playfully bit it and he smiled.

"I'm married to a woman that I don't love anymore. She doesn't give a fuck about me or my son. I've been with her for a long time now. I won't go into details, but just know that we're over. I'm not lying to you either, Sophie, because I don't have to. If I wanted a mistress I could easily find one. I'm just through with her. You caught my eye and what I want to do right now is save you." His words could have had good intentions, but they pissed me off. I gently pushed his hand away that was still on my cheek and looked at him.

"Ameer, I don't need saving. I'm doing just fine," I said very offended by his words.

Ameer cocked his head to the side and frowned.

"I didn't mean it like that, but what if I did? People miss out on blessings being prideful. I see you dealing with your wild ass sister and living in that small ass apartment. Erin told me about your parents and I'm sorry that happened to y'all. How were you able to keep them? How old are you?" he asked.

"19 and my godfather helped me. He's the only person that I know I can count on."

Ameer frowned like my words angered him.

"Your parents didn't have family?"

"My mother's family lives in Minnesota and my father's family never really cared for us. They hated my mother from the start because she wasn't wealthy like my dad."

Ameer nodded and looked at me the same way Johnny did. I didn't want Ameer to pity us. Things were bad, but they would get better. They had to.

"I like you, Sophie, and I want to help. Whether you get with me or not, I'm a help you out because I'm that kind of nigga," he said sincerely and he grabbed my hand. The fact that he always needed to touch me made me smile. He was slowly wearing me down.

"Ameer, what do you want from me? I have so much going on in my life. I don't need your drama and you know this."

Ameer nodded and he sighed.

"Shit, don't I know it, but I'm a selfish nigga and I have to have you. I feel like you need me just as much as I need you. I'm not going anywhere and you should just stop fighting it. From here on out, I'm a make sure you and your sisters is straight. I'm a hold you down ma."

I laughed and looked at him. Marcus had once said the same thing to me and he hurt me like he had never loved me at all.

"Yeah, okay."

Ameer smiled and grabbed my face with both of his hands. He leaned towards me and gently kissed my lips while looking into my eyes. The emotions that he showed me in them caused me to moan. He couldn't possibly feel anything for me. Hell, he didn't even know me. I pulled away from him scared that the girls or Ahmad would run over and he bit my lip playfully. He smiled and looked me in the eyes.

"You going to be loving a nigga in a minute," he said in a matter of fact kind of way. I smiled, but ignored what he said. He would take me and the girls home and I would find a way to dodge him until he got tired of chasing me. I wasn't leading him on; I just didn't have time for the games. He said he was through with his wife, but how was I to know what he was saying was true. Married men didn't leave their wives is what I'd always heard and I wasn't going to hype myself on promises that I was for sure would be broken.

After letting the girls and Ahmad play another hour, we went back to my place. I laid Ahmad down in my bed while the girls went to their room that was across from mines. Ameer walked up behind me as I watched Ahmad sleep. He was so cute and I had already grown attached to him.

"Ma, I got you. Just let me be there for you. I won't rest well until I know you and your sisters is doing better than this."

My tears fell freely as I thought about just how tight

things were for me. I sighed and wiped them away. The girls and I didn't have much, but we had each other. I walked out of the room and Ameer followed me into the living room. We sat down on the couch and Ameer pulled me to his side. He grabbed my remote and looked at my television.

"See my now this that shit I don't like. I can't even fucking see the screen," he complained with a smile. My television was a 32-inch flat screen. To me it was fine, but I guess to a *boss* like him it wasn't good enough. Maybe he had 80 inches sitting in every room in his house. I had too much on my mind I didn't care about the size of a damn television.

"Ameer, I'm more worried about what we're going to eat. Fuck a TV."

Ameer sighed and pulled me onto his lap. All day the sexual tension between us had been slowly building. His hands went to my hips and then up my back. He leaned towards me and pulled my bottom lip into his mouth. My sex was throbbing. I slowly grinded on him and he looked at me.

"Sophie, don't do that. I'm hard as fuck and we can't do shit on this little ass couch."

I laughed and he kissed me again. His hands went to my breast and he massaged them. He tweaked my nipples through my bra and I moaned in his mouth. My head fell back and he started to lick and suck on my neck. I heard Drew laughing at something while in her bedroom and my lusty haze washed away. I sat up straight and slowly peeled myself off of Ameer. He grabbed my hand and placed it on top of his massive erection. I looked down at the big imprint and then up at him. His sexy hazel eyes were heavy with lust.

"You won't be able to get away next time ma."

I licked my lips and exhaled. My damn heart was beating a mile a minute. I was so horny I couldn't think straight. I wanted and needed him inside of me.

"Ameer, it won't be a next time."

Ameer grabbed the remote from off the floor where it had fallen to and he smiled.

"Yeah, okay."

I leaned back and watched him flick through channels. It couldn't be a next time because no matter how nice today was, I still didn't know if I could trust him and I wasn't going to stick around to find out.

Chapter Eight

Ameer

It took me four fucking weeks to break Sophie down. Four weeks like what the fuck, but she finally saw that I wasn't playing and now I was trying to do some even more slick shit to make us official. I had Princeton run up in her crib and set a controlled fire. He put it out once most of her stuff was fucked up so that it didn't spread to the rest of the units and now I was waiting on her to call me crying. The shit sounded fucked up, but a nigga had good intentions.

Princeton was sitting next to me and Aamil was in the back seat. They thought the shit was funny, but I didn't care. Sophie was special and different than any other woman that I had met. Yeah, I was 11 years older than her, but I couldn't let her get away. She had been through so much and she still found a reason to smile. I had seen niggas crumble under way less stress. I was intrigued by her. I wasn't going to be happy until I had her in my bed every night and so that was what I did. Found a way to get her to move into my new home with me. A place that Tatum didn't even know about.

"So, let me get this straight. You had Princeton set a fire to her place so that you could move her onto the compound that you've never even took Tatum to?" Aamil asked.

I took a sip of my lean and nodded. Aamil started laughing and Princeton joined in with him. I looked at both of them single ass niggas and shook my head. They wouldn't understand. They could fuck with different chicks and be cool going home to a cold ass bed. I was tired of sleeping alone and Sophie was the first real woman that I had come across in a long time. I didn't want to let her pass. Shit, I wasn't going to let her pass.

I knew that the shit I was doing was wrong, but I didn't

give a fuck. Tatum was on the way out and Sophie was on the way in. I just needed to holler at my lawyer and have him give Luke the divorce papers. Tatum would put up a fight, but I would find a way to make her sign. Money was her God and I knew just how to get her out of my life. Cut her a check.

"Y'all might think the shit funny, but I don't really give a fuck. Sophie is cool as hell and she's a good person. Plus she's fine as fuck. It's time for Tatum to get the fuck on and never come back."

Princeton looked at me and smiled.

"And what is Tatum going to say about all of this? You know Sophie can't handle Tatum. She look like she can bang, but Tatum would rip her fucking head off of her shoulders."

I shook my head and took another sip of my lean. I didn't usually get faded, but I was anxious to have Sophie living with me and I needed something to calm my nerves.

"She won't have to handle her. I'll handle Tatum and if she touches Sophie I'm a fuck her up," I said and meant every word.

Princeton and Aamil laughed some more. Aamil started choking from laughing so hard. That was what his bitch ass got for laughing at me.

"Shit, what the pussy do? She got you playing Tatum to the left and shit. I'm happy as hell to see Tatum's trifling ass go, but I'm still shocked that you so into Sophie. She must be a pro in the bedroom," Aamil said.

I cleared my throat and looked down at my ringing phone. Once I answered this question, those niggas was going to really clown me. I declined Tatum's call and looked out of the window at Sophie's job.

"I wouldn't know, we haven't fucked yet."

"WHAT!" Aamil yelled loud as hell. Princeton started laughing and my cellphone started ringing again. I looked down at Sophie's name and held my hand up. The whole car got quiet.

"What up bae?"

She sniffled on the other end of the phone and I smiled. Got her! I hated to hear her crying, but I would kiss her and take all that pain away.

"My landlord just called me and said that my apartment caught on fire. I don't know what to do, Ameer. Janelle has done so much for me already, I don't feel right going to stay with her plus she's been acting distant lately. I'm thinking about getting a room for a few days."

I sighed and rubbed my beard.

"Sophie, why would you get a room when you have me? That place I told you about is ready. That can be our home that we stay in together baby. You, me, the girls and Ahmad."

Sophie was quiet for a long time then she exhaled on the other end of the phone and I knew I had her.

"Okay, I mean…wait where would your wife be at?"

The mention of the word "wife" upset me, but I wasn't going to let that fuck up my mood. Tatum wasn't my damn wife. On paper yes, but morally no. She hadn't acted like my wife in a long damn time and now it was too late. Life didn't wait on you to get your shit together. She had her chance and she blew it. I had been nothing but good to her. She pushed me away.

"Don't worry about her. I'll pick you up and then we can grab the girls. I got this ma. Remember what I said?" I asked. I didn't want to get all soft and shit in front of my brothers, but really I didn't give a fuck. Sophie brought emotions out of me that Tatum never had. It was crazy and I had started questioning if I was ever truly in love with Tatum to begin with.

"Yes, I remember," Sophie replied in that sweet ass voice of hers.

"And what was that?" I asked looking out of the window.

Sophie sighed. "That with you by my side I won't need anyone else because you were going to hold me down."

I smiled and licked my lips. I couldn't wait to get ahold of her.

"Exactly, so stop tripping like you didn't know who your nigga was. I'll be at your job in ten." I ended the call and Aamil chuckled. This nigga.

"*Remember what I said? Tell me you love me Sophie please baby*," he said trying to be funny and shit. I shook my head at his silly ass and we all started laughing.

I called Luke and he answered on the first ring.

"Aye, Luke everything's a go. I'mma grab Sophie and her sisters now. We'll get Ahmad from Aunt Saniyah's, too, so you don't have to go get him."

Luke chuckled and I already knew what he was about to say.

"Alright, Ameer, I'm happy to see you getting rid of Tatum."

I laughed.

"Yeah, I am, Luke. Make sure the house is ready for us."

I ended the call and got comfortable in my seat.

"So, what's the word on Floyd?" His bitch ass was still in hiding.

Aamil groaned, but out the corner of my eyes I noticed Princeton smile.

"I got his side bitch at the spot in Highland Park. We waiting to see when Floyd is going to call her. We had her text him that she was staying at her friends for a while because her house was getting re-painted and he responded okay. I mean I don't think he's going to call, but we'll see. What you want me to do with her if he doesn't call?"

"Kill her," Aamil said without giving it a second thought. Princeton looked at me and I nodded. Shit I didn't give a fuck about Floyd's side bitch and he wouldn't give two fucks about mine.

"Alright, I'll give that nigga another week and if he doesn't call, I'll take care of her. She a trick anyway. I knew two dudes that she set up for Floyd and he killed them and took they work," Princeton said.

"See we're doing the city a favor by taking her out. A sneaky bitch deserves to die," Aamil said and laughed.

"Yeah, but anyway we gotta get this nigga. I found this address that I think is his grandmother's. I'm a put Reem and Bucks on it and see what pops up. It's deep into the burbs, so they gotta be low-key, but I got a good feeling about it. If we could granny to give him a call then his ass would be straight bitch made if he didn't give himself up," I said and smiled.

"Hell yeah, but he is a grimy nigga. I wouldn't put anything past his ass," Aamil chimed in.

"You gotta get him before pops do, Aamil. I'm ready to chill and just collect this easy money. You want the top spot, so you gotta put that work in nigga. Are you going to catch up with him before uncle Hashim or Mason does?"

"I said I would. I got a lot of shit on my plate, but getting this nigga is my number one priority, Ameer, so calm the fuck down," he replied with an attitude. I wondered what the fuck he had on his plate as I watched Sophie exit the jewelry store. She looked around for my truck, but I wasn't in it. I rode with Princeton. I rolled the window down and her eyes locked with mine. She gave me a small smile and headed my way.

Sophie was so fucking beautiful and what made her even more attractive was that she didn't know it. I mean she had confidence, but I could tell it had dwindled down because of some dumb nigga that didn't know what he had. Sophie was average height around 5'6 with a banging ass body. Thick hips with even juicer thighs and the perfect sized breasts. Sophie had a chunky face, which was sexy as hell on her because I loved a chick with dimples. Slanted eyes that mainly Asian women were known for, but Sophie was all black and she was beautiful.

I noticed Princeton and Aamil checking her out in her tight black knee length skirt and 6-inch heels. I glared at them niggas before opening the door.

"Eyes on the floor motherfuckers," I said only half joking. Sophie ran into my arms and I hugged her tight. I looked down at her face and smiled at her. Her eyes were glossy and her lips were stained from red lipstick. I bent down to kiss her and I heard tires screeching. I threw Sophie into the truck and before I could jump in myself the sound of gunfire filled my ears. A bullet pierced my side and then one hit my leg.

Princeton pulled me into the truck as Aamil shot out of

his window. The gunshots died down as the car sped away. I laid on my side and closed my eyes.

"Ameer, are you okay baby?" Sophie asked touching the side of my face. I tried to look up and Aamil pushed my head down. Princeton pulled off and started driving fast as hell down the street.

"Don't move nigga!" Princeton yelled.

I could hear Sophie crying and the shit had me all fucked up. From the moment I stepped into her life, I had been nothing but fucking trouble.

Chapter Nine

Princeton

I took Ameer to my nigga Buck's father's house who was also a surgeon and we took him downstairs to his surgery room. Buck's father was making good money at the hospital, but that didn't stop him from taking money from us whenever we called. Only a fool would turn down the stacks that we were offering him.

Aamil sat across from me on his phone with Kasam and Sophie sat next to me with a tear stained face looking so beautiful. If her ass had talked to me she wouldn't be going through any of this right now. Yeah, my niggas lived a chaotic life, but my own personal life was very stress free. I grabbed Sophie's hand not really thinking about it and started rubbing the back of it. She gave me a weak smile and leaned her head on my shoulder.

Aamil glanced our way, but didn't say anything. I wasn't trying to get with her. I had accepted the fact that she was now with Ameer and I was cool with that. Ameer was a cool nigga and Tatum really was a bitch, so I was happy for him. My phone started vibrating in my pocket and Sophie sat her head up. I stopped rubbing her hand and stood up. I knew who was calling and what they wanted.

Life was all about decisions. One fucking mistake had altered my damn life and I didn't know how to turn the shit around. I fucked up and I was now paying for the shit. I walked up the stairs and out the side door of the house. I checked around for Luke's old sneaky ass before calling back the number. Of course he answered on the first ring.

"I heard that Ameer was shot twice. Is it true?" he asked.

I leaned against the house and checked around for somebody once more. People were always lurking.

"Yeah, he's good," I answered in a low voice.

"Well, did you shoot him?"

"Hell no, I didn't. I told you that I wouldn't do that. You'll have to find another way for me to help you," I told him.

He laughed.

"Nigga, I didn't fuck my best friend's wife and her damn girlfriend. You're not in a position to turn down shit. I said for you to find a way for them bitches to be 6-feet under. The clock is ticking motherfucker or he will be getting that video and well you know what happens after that." The call ended and a throat cleared from behind me. I turned around and Luke was standing behind me smoking a cigarette.

Luke was like a fucking superhero or some shit. He always popping up out of the blue. I looked around for the cloud of smoke that he came out of. I never saw the nigga do anything other than watch Ameer's fucking back. I put my phone away and nodded to him.

"You good, Luke?"

Luke sighed. He was a big nigga and had to weigh a lot. I would have to pump him full of fucking bullets and I lifted over 250 pound, so I wasn't little, but this nigga was not the person you wanted to fight. You shoot his ass and you shoot to kill. Fuck an injury. Death and hot bullets was the only thing I would leave Luke with.

"Yeah, I'm good. I had Saniyah get the kids, so that I could come check out Ameer. What happened?"

I stood up straight and looked him in the eyes. I didn't have shit to hide, but being around him always made me feel uneasy for some reason.

"Shit, we were sitting outside of Sophie's job. She walked over to the truck and somebody drove by dumping. The shit was crazy."

Luke pressed his lips together and tossed his cigarette into the bushes. He fixed the button on his suit jacket and looked up at me. No matter what the weather was this nigga always had on a fucking suit if the nigga wasn't so intimidating his ass would be comical.

"I'll handle it. It's some shit happening within the camp."

His eyes seemed to bore into me as he said it. Either I was just being paranoid or this nigga new something. I was going to have to find a way to get rid of his ass. I loved Luke. He had always been in Ameer's life and was nothing but nice to me but if it came down to him or me it would always be me.

"Oh yeah? Is it something I need to know Luke?" I asked with an attitude so that he could think I was concerned about a possible snitch.

Luke smiled, something his ass didn't do often.

"Princeton, I've got it covered. Go be with your friend and check on Sophie. She loves Ameer, so you should be there for her and let her know he's going to be fine. You know that right?"

I shrugged. Shit I had no clue what the nigga was talking about.

"I mean you do know Ameer is going to be fine and that Sophie loves him?" he asked. I stared at his ass and we glared at each other for a moment. I didn't want to reach for my shit because then he would know that I was guilty of something, but I had a feeling he was about to shoot my ass. My hand casually veered towards the back and Luke started laughing. He hit my arm playfully and looked at me.

"Princeton, you could never take a joke. Go check on your boy and I'll be out here guarding the house."

I smiled relieved as hell that he was just playing and I walked off. I found Sophie downstairs sitting next to Aamil.

She was laying her head on his shoulder and he was showing her something on his phone. That shit pissed me the fuck off. I mean if I couldn't be with her then the least I could do was console her. Sophie looked at me and she wiped her wet eyes.

"You good?" she asked.

I sat back down in my original seat and Aamil looked over at me. He looked like Ameer and Kasam, but then he didn't. The shit was weird. Aamil was dark as fuck with this silky ass hair and then his eyes were different than theirs, too. I always wondered what was up with that, but whatever. Ma wouldn't do that shit. She'd have to have a death wish to cheat on Shadid Matin. That nigga had built along with Mason a very lucrative drug empire. Who knows how much the nigga was worth, but I knew it was millions and shit Mason was fore sure a billionaire.

"Yeah, I'm good," I said to Sophie looking back at her.

Sophie looked at me with those damn slanted eyes and she smiled. She was so beautiful.

"Are you sure?" she asked. I nodded and looked away from her. I couldn't stare too long at her with Aamil around. His ass saw everything and I didn't need no beef with him in my life. I had enough shit to worry about like how I was going to handle the motherfucker blackmailing me. There was no way in hell I was going to set up Ameer and his brothers. Those niggas were the only family I had left.

I wanted to just kill this nigga, but he kept a gang of motherfuckers around him. I knew where he stayed at, but I couldn't get into that bitch by myself. I was close with Reem, but once he found out the details of this shit, he would turn on me. I had no clue what the fuck I was going to do.

An hour later, Aamil had me take Sophie to the compound. Yeah, the nigga really had a fucking compound and shit. Only niggas I knew with shit like this was leaders of cartels. Ameer's ass was crazy. Living like he fucking Pablo Escobar and shit. I loved Ameer like a brother, but this shit was really starting to go to his head. Security cleared me to come in and I drove to Ameer's house. He also had a house for his moms in here and houses for his brothers. I guess the nigga forgot about me.

I pulled my truck up into his driveway and I parked. Sophie was asleep leaning against the car window and looking so damn sexy in her work clothes. I traced the outline of her hip with my finger. When she didn't move, I touched her ass. I couldn't help it and man wasn't that shit soft! I bit down on my lip and groaned. I looked around and only saw a few guards on their post, but nobody was looking our way. I gently rubbed her arm to wake her up.

"Sophie, get up ma."

Sophie continued to sleep. I got out of the truck and walked around to her side. I slowly pulled Sophie out and carried her into the house. I smiled at the maid that opened the door for us and I carried Sophie upstairs to the room that she would now be sharing with Aamil. That shit was fly as hell I couldn't even hate if I wanted to. This nigga had too much money and I was living in a damn townhouse. That shit made me mad.

I laid Sophie in the center of the bed and she rolled onto her side. I looked behind me and then back at Sophie. Something clicked in me and I just had to have a little more time with her. I climbed onto the bed and kissed her shoulder. She moaned and grinded onto my dick.

"What the fuck are you doing?"

I jumped up and looked at the door. My gun was in my hand and I was breathing hard as hell. Drew's little ass was standing in the door smiling at me. I let out that damn breath I was holding in and put my gun away. I walked over to her and grabbed her face. She was my little hitta for sure, but the bitch didn't know how to talk to people.

"Bitch don't be sneaking up on me."

Drew smiled and licked her full lips. She was bad as hell. Slim with big breast and a plump ass. Not to mention a freak.

"Let me find out you crushing on Sophie. Ameer going to fuck you up," she said and smiled. I let go of her face and I walked past her. I led Drew to her bedroom and we walked in. I shut the door behind us and locked it. I didn't need anyone walking in on us. Drew walked over to the bed and I looked at her. She was wild as hell, but I liked that. She wasn't Sophie and shit she didn't even look as good as Erin, but she wasn't ugly. She was setting niggas up for me and everything.

"I called you five times today and you didn't answer. Where was you at?" I asked walking over to her.

"Out until Erin caught up with me and told me about the apartment. I'm not your bi…"

I cut her off slapping the shit out of her. I grabbed a handful of her hair and looked down at her. I was never big on beating women, but she pulled the worst up out of a nigga. Shit I had blacked her eye not too long ago because I found out she was fucking with this eastside nigga name Tommy. I didn't play that shit. I was the one to pop that cherry and so her shit would forever belong to me.

"Drew, watch what the fuck you say to me. If I call your fucking phone you answer it. The shit isn't rocket science." Drew nodded and I let her hair go. While looking down at Drew, I got a good ass idea. I rubbed her cheek that I had just slapped and dropped to my knees. I placed my hands onto her thigh and looked at her.

"You my bitch, Drew. I can't have you out her fucking with niggas. That shit would have me looking bad as hell."

"But people don't even know where together, Princeton."

I smiled and started to pull her leggings off.

"But I do and when you turn 18, I'll tell everybody. I got somebody new that I need you to help me get baby. You going to ride for your nigga?" I asked sticking two fingers inside of her. Drew moaned and fell back onto the bed. I stood up and continued to finger her.

"He's a big timer baby, so it's going to take some time, but I know you can get his ass. I got a plan and I know it can work. I just need you to be with me on this. We take this nigga out and the city will be ours."

I sped up my movements and Drew's legs started to shake. I reached for her breast and started to massage her nipples through her tank top.

"Are you going to help me baby?" I asked and stopped moving my fingers. Drew looked up at me and she smiled.

"Nigga yes now finish what the fuck you was doing."

I smiled wanting to slap the shit out of her, but I finished her off. I dropped my pants and climbed onto the bed. I would fuck her real quick. Run the plan by her and then I would bounce before Luke's ass came home. If shit went right, I would be the next one on the throne instead of Aamil. Shit he didn't want that shit as bad as I did anyway. I was willing to put in that work.

Chapter Ten

Drew

I laid in bed after Princeton left feeling like a million bucks. Erin slowly walked into the room not even having enough fucking manners to knock and looked at me. I hated her ass because she was just like Sophie. A fucking goody two shoes type bitch. I didn't have the time nor the patience to act like I was the perfect girl for niggas. Either they was going to like me how I was or they could get the fuck on. That was why I liked Princeton. He didn't try to change or tame me. Plus he stayed cashing me out and was paid out the ass. How could you not like a nigga like that?

"You foul as hell. Sophie has finally found someone that makes her happy and you do this. What the fuck is wrong with you?" Erin asked. I looked at her and I rolled my eyes. Erin was thick as hell like Sophie only she kept her hair straightened at all times and had dyed it this ugly ass brown. She looked just like mom and even that made me mad. Why couldn't I look like her? Why Erin? That bitch didn't deserve to look like her if I didn't.

"Don't knock it until you try it. Aamil and Kasam will be walking around here soon enough, bitch you better pick one or hell fuck them both we only live once," I said and laughed. I grabbed a blunt off of my dresser and lit it up. Erin was a goody two shoes but even she couldn't turn away that Kush. She walked over to the bed and sat down. Her hair was braided into one big side braid like mom used to do and I got teary-eyed looking at her. I took a few pulls of the blunt before passing it to her.

"But for real Sophie lucked up with this nigga Ameer. We back like we never left and living better than ever. I just know this nigga is about to be cashing us out bitch," I said excited at the thought of getting a car and expensive clothes.

Shit we had before my dad flipped the fuck out. Erin handed me back the blunt and she shook her head. I hated that she was more like Sophie than me. We could have been setting niggas up together and getting real money.

"Drew, it's not about the money. I'm just happy that Sophie's found someone that treats her right. Then what makes it better is that we get to have Ahmad in our lives. I love him already," she said and smiled. I nodded with a big ass grin on my face because I loved his little bad ass, too. I thought about his mother and frowned.

"And what if his momma come up in here talking shit? I mean she is married to Ameer. This shit is crazy."

Erin took the blunt from me and took two pulls before handing it back. I put it out and Erin sighed.

"If I was her I would be mad as fuck but she not about to do shit to us or Sophie. I would beat her ass," she said looking me straight in the eyes and I believed her. Erin was a lot of things and a punk wasn't one of them. That's why I never really fought her like that because the bitch could bang. She had the worst fucking temper. She didn't say much, but she would fuck some shit up.

"So, you sleeping with Princeton?" she asked. I nodded

and waited for her to lecture me, but it never came. She smiled and stood up.

"I mean I get it, he is really sexy, but don't get caught up in him. Think with your mind and not your heart. Don't mess this up for Sophie. I can tell she really likes Ameer maybe even love him. She deserves to be happy." Erin smiled at me and walked out of the room. I laid back in the bed and looked up at the ceiling. It was always about Sophie and how good she was or what she was sacrificing. What about me? I deserved happiness and that was Princeton. He was planning some wild ass shit, but I was down with it. He was the only person holding me down and so why wouldn't I hold him down?

Chapter Eleven

Tatum

I couldn't stop laughing as Nina drove to her house. I had followed Ameer to his new bitch's job and I just couldn't take seeing him hug her and shit. The way he looked down at her broke my fucking heart. He used to look at me that way, but now all I got was a few fucking dollars and a quick fuck. That nigga had me fucked up if he thought I was going to let that shit slide. Fuck that. Nina handed me her gun and I let that bitch go as we rolled by them. When I saw Ameer fall I damn near shot myself. I wasn't trying to shoot him, but oh well. He'd just think it was Floyd trying to get at him anyway.

"That shit was funny as hell!" Nina yelled.

I laughed and smiled, but all I could think about was if Ameer was okay. I still loved him and I wanted to try to make things work with him. I just had to get that Ashanti looking bitch out of the way.

"Yeah, but I wish I could have shot that broccoli headed bitch." I said and rolled my eyes.

Nina looked over at me and she laughed.

"Yeah, that bitch does have some wild looking ass long hair, but her body was on point. Shit with an ass like that you should be trying to do a threesome with them."

I frowned and shook my head. This was exactly why Nina didn't have a fucking man.

"Nina, I am not about to do that shit with somebody he cares about. And watch him fuck her like he loves her and shit? Hell no!" I shouted pissed that she would suggest some bullshit like that in the first place.

Nina rubbed my thigh and her hand moved to between my legs. She started to massage my pussy through my jeans and I moaned.

"Calm down boo you know I was just playing. Now, let's go spend some of your man's hard earned money. After I eat you out better than he ever could you can go home and see if he's okay," she said while continuing to massage me through my jeans. I nodded and she headed to the mall. I called Ameer several times as we went in and out of stores spending money that I had stolen out of his safe the day before, but he didn't pick up. I called Aamil and he answered on the first ring.

"What up, Tate?" he asked calling me by the nickname he gave me.

I watched Nina spend $2,000 on a Fendi bag and I sighed. This bitch had that same bag in blue. With Ameer only giving me $2,000 a week. I couldn't shop like that anymore and that pissed me off. I could blow $15,000 in one store.

"Nothing shopping, where is your brother?"

"Shopping? Bitch your husband was fucking shot twice and you out shopping. Delete my number it was nice knowing you." Aamil ended the call and I looked at Nina. She was grabbing her change from the cashier. She saw my frown and stopped smiling.

"What's wrong?"

I shook my head and tried to call Saniyah. For some reason, I wanted to see Ahmad really bad. I hadn't been home in weeks and I actually fucking missed him. Saniyah sent me to voicemail and then so did every other number that I called that was connected to Ameer. I bought a few more things before rushing home to see what the hell was going on. Did he die or some shit?

****

I walked into my house a few hours later high off a molly and worried about Ameer. I looked around and noticed that all of the guards were gone except for Luke. He sat at my dining room table with a mean as mug on his face. He never liked me and I never liked him; the feeling was mutual.

"Luke, where is Ahmad and Ameer?"

Luke looked up at me.

"Now you care?"

I frowned and cocked my head to the side.

"Nigga, you better watch what the fuck you say to me."

Luke laughed and tapped his finger on a stack of papers.

"Tatum, I never liked you and I can't even begin to express how happy I am to see you go. You have two fucking options and so you better make the right fucking choice. Sign these divorce and custody papers and you will get to keep this house along with a monthly alimony check of $40,000. Don't sign them and you won't get shit. Back to your momma house you go," he said while looking at me.

I licked my lips because I had cottonmouth like a motherfucker and wondered if this was some kind of sick joke. I mean, did he know that it was me who shot Ameer? But then I shook that thought of out my head because if he did then I would have been dead already.

"Luke, where the fuck is Ameer?"

Luke stopped tapping the papers and sat up straight in his seat. He was a big man and was all muscles with a low cut fade and no facial hair except for a thin mustache. I wouldn't admit it out loud, but he scared the fuck out of me.

"I was trying to be nice, but you testing my fucking patience. Sign these damn papers or get out. No money, no cars, and no house. The good life gone like that."

My eyes watered as all of my worst fears came to life. Damn. After ten years, I never thought he would play me like this. Ameer was a foul motherfucker for real.

"I'm not signing shit! Get the fuck out of my house, Luke, and tell Ameer to come to me like a fucking man and ask me for a divorce," I said knowing he wasn't in a position to ask for me shit right about now.

Luke stood up and walked over to me. Before I could run, he picked me up and tossed me over his shoulder. He pulled the house keys out of my pocket and grabbed my purse. I kicked and screamed as Luke opened my double doors and tossed me onto the cobblestone like I was a piece of fucking trash.

I rubbed my scratched up elbow and looked up at Luke. This was some straight bullshit.

"Luke, this is my house! I'll call the cops!" I yelled.

Luke's face was void of emotion as he went through my purse. I watched him take all of my credit cards and money out of it. He tossed me my license and my cellphone.

"You want some stability sign them papers until then you own your own." He looked down at me and shook his head before closing the door.

I slowly stood up and called Ameer's cellphone. He answered on the first ring. I heard a bitch giggling in the background and my blood turned to fire I was so fucking mad.

"Who is that bitch and why are you treating me like this?"

"Ma' Ameer was shot today and he's doped up on medicine. He's done with you and well you know how it goes. What he says goes and so you have no reason to call him anymore. Until Ameer says otherwise, you dead to us." Reem ended the call and I saw my whole life flash before my eyes. My wedding day, the birth of my son. Ameer and I making love. All that happiness we once shared was now gone.

I whimpered and the tears started to fall. That nigga had canceled me like I wasn't shit to him. Like I wasn't his wife and the mother of his son. He had me fucked up. He would pay for this shit and I swear it would be in the worst fucking way. I called the one person that I knew would be happy to hear from me and he answered on the first ring.

"Tatum, where you at I miss you bae?" he said. I slowly stood up and walked away from my dream home.

"Stuck in Northville. Can you come get me from a gas station?" I asked walking out of my driveway. I would have let him come to the house, but what was the point? If Ameer had kicked me out then that meant he had a new crib and wouldn't be back to this house anytime soon.

"Bet I got you. Is that nigga with you?"

I rubbed my scratched up elbow again and I started to

cry. This was some fucked up shit.

"No, he isn't nigga, just meet me at the gas station off of 7mile and Beck Road." I ended the call and headed for the gas station. I would give Ameer one chance to get me back and if that nigga acted like he was really finished with me then I would send Floyd straight to his brother's house. I should have been the last bitch he wanted to make mad.

Chapter Twelve

Janelle

"So, where is she at then?" my dad yelled. He paced his office with his hands in his pockets. Sophie had been missing in action for weeks now and he was pissed. She had quit her job and wasn't answering any of our calls. Dad was going crazy not being able to talk to her. I shook my head tired of hearing this damn speech and looked at him.

"Dad she is with that dope dealer. He's bad news, but if that's who she wants then so be it," I said with a smile on my face to piss him off. I wasn't stupid I knew that my father put Sophie on a pedestal and it irked me to know that he loved her more than me.

"Janelle, I care for those girls and it is my responsibility to look after them. I promised your mother that I would," he said with sad eyes. Whenever he talked about Sophie, he got all emotional. I loved Sophie like a sister, but I wasn't going to beg her to be around us. Being with Ameer had obviously gone to her damn head. We were there for her when she didn't have shit and now that she was seeing some money again she was too good for us? I would wait for him to toss her to the side and I knew she would be back.

"Well, I don't know what you want me to do," I said as my cellphone vibrated in my lap. I looked at the screen and smiled when I saw Floyd's name pop up. I silenced his call and looked up at my father. "Look, I have to go. If I can get her to pick up the phone then I will tell her that you're trying to get in contact with her. Really it's no use though. She's head over heels in love with him. I'm just sad because the girls deserve more. We all know he isn't going to divorce his wife."

My dad sighed and shook his head. He walked over to me and kissed both of my cheeks.

"Okay, well at least try to get her to pick up. Tell her I love, her too." He smiled and walked away. If only he would have looked at me for a second longer he would have saw the pain and hurt that his words caused. Not once had my father told me he loved me. Whenever I would tell him that I loved him, he would say me too and act like things were all good. He was always concerned about Sophie and not giving two fucks about me.

I pulled my emotions together and walked out of his office. Fuck him and fuck Sophie. The bitch not only had Ameer, now she had my dad fucking chasing after her. What made her so fucking special?

****

After leaving my dad's office, I drove to a hotel in Ann Arbor to meet up with Floyd. I met him at my job last week. He came in asking for Sophie and I ended up riding him on my swivel chair. He was fine as hell and I was willing to keep him as a cuddle buddy until Kasam came back to the states. He was touring in Europe and avoiding me, but once he knew what I was about to do for him, he would have to wife me.

I heard from my girls at the beauty shop that Floyd was beefing with the Matin family. Sophie was clueless as hell when it came to the dope boys, but I wasn't. I knew who Princeton was when he walked into my shop. I just had to play it off. I didn't want to come off as a groupie or something.

I could have easily gotten a corporate man, but I didn't want one. For one all of the men that I knew that was really pulling in money had a white woman on their arm and the other ones were just too damn boring for me. I liked the unexpected. I couldn't do the same routine with a man day in and day out. Being with a dope boy gave me the excitement that my life was lacking. Now, if only I could get one of them to fall in love with me.

Love me how my father loved Sophie then I would be happy. So I devised a plan that would have Kasam eating out the palm of my hand. If I helped him take down Floyd, he would have to show me some love. Once I became his number one go to girl, then I would do what I had to do to get pregnant. Busting condoms, turkey basting, you name it and I would try it all until I got what I wanted.

I grabbed my hotel key from the girl at the front desk

and went up to the penthouse. I had to give it to Floyd; he knew how to stay off the radar. If he wasn't so damn crazy I would have tried to get him to fall in love with me, but I could tell he was after me for one reason and well I was after him for a purpose, too. I would play my part and set his ass up when the time came.

Once I stepped off of the elevator, I spotted two men in jeans and hoodies standing near the first door to my right. Either he was being extra careful or he was scared as hell of Kasam and his brothers. I smiled at the guards and handed them the key. They looked me up and down and knocked on the door. It opened minutes later and Floyd stood on the other end of the door.

He was wearing nothing but a towel and looking so damn good. Floyd was around 6'1 with a fit athletic body. A couple of tattoos and a cute face. He didn't look better than Kasam, but he wasn't bad to look at either. He had short curly hair that was tapered with a mustache. I walked up on him and he kissed me gently on the lips. He grabbed me by the hand and pulled me into the hotel room. Just thinking about sex with him had me wet.

"So, what's going on sweetie?" I asked looking around

his room. It was big but nothing I hadn't seen before. I clutched my purse tightly to me. It held the tracking device that I was going to plant on him in it. It was a small black chip that he wouldn't even feel when I placed it into his wallet.

"Nothing, I just wanted to see what was up with you beautiful. You rode a nigga like you was going for broke and now you surprised that I wanted more?" he asked me with a smile. I smiled at him and followed him into the bedroom. He led me over to the bed and I sat at the edge. Floyd pulled off my shoes and rubbed his hands up and down my legs.

"Do you want something to drink, Janelle?" he asked looking up at me. He seemed a little different from the last time I saw him, but since I didn't know him that well I shook it off. I nodded and he gave me a quick kiss before standing up and walking away.

I slipped off my black-cropped jacket and waited for Floyd to return. He walked back in a few minutes later with two glasses of peach colored liquor. He handed me a glass and sat down next to me. I looked to the left of the room and almost jumped out of my skin when I saw this tall brown skin man sitting in a chair with a shotgun on his lap. Floyd chuckled and kissed me on the neck.

"Forget he's even here beautiful. Let's toast to new friendships," Floyd said in a low voice and sucked my ear into his mouth. I downed the drink, which was Cîroc and peach juice and looked at Floyd. He took a sip of his drink and sat both of our glasses onto the nightstand. I began to take off my clothes anticipating him sliding up inside of me. His hooded eyes devoured me and I was getting so horny I could barely think straight. I took a step towards him and my legs wobbled. I smiled and licked my lips.

"I'm buzzing already," I said to him.

Floyd chuckled. He pulled off his towel and his big dick swayed back and forth. It was so beautiful it deserved its own name. I licked my lips as I threw my thongs across the room. Floyd put on a condom and I climbed onto the bed. Floyd grabbed a belt and I looked at him.

"What are you about to do with that?" I asked not feeling no bdsm type shit. Floyd ignored me and climbed onto the bed. He sat on my legs and looked down at me. It was then that I noticed he had Tatum tattooed over his heart.

"I'm into all kinds of shit beautiful. I'm a wrap this belt around your neck and I swear when you come that shit is going to feel amazing," he said. I looked at the thick belt and then up at him. He was smiling at me with lust filled eyes and it made me feel good to be the woman that he wanted to do this with. What could go wrong? Hell I liked a good orgasm. I nodded and lifted my head. Floyd placed the belt around it and pulled it as tight as it would go. My air circulation was instantly cut off. I clawed at the belt and the tall guy jumped up. He pumped the shotgun and pointed it at my head. Floyd laughed and loosened his grip on the belt.

He opened my legs and slammed his penis inside of me. I cried out and he tightened the grip on the belt.

"Just relax and you will like it ma," he said with a smile on his face. He was fucking certified crazy. He eventually loosened the grip on the belt and I panted for air.

"Where is your friend Sophie at?" he asked.

I shook my head not knowing what to say. The question had caught me all off guard. Floyd began to move in and out of me and he was hard as a brick. I think this shit was really turning him on.

"You not fucking with me to set me up are you?"

"No, why would I do that?" I asked as innocent as I possibly could. Floyd stopped smiling and slapped me so hard across the face I saw stars literally. He hiked my legs up onto his shoulders and began to fuck me so hard I couldn't do anything other than look at him. He was hitting me deep in my stomach. The shit was crazy. I could feel him jerk inside of me and I thanked God. I had to think of a way to get out of this room. This had gone nothing like I had imagined it would. Floyd pulled out of me, but stayed between my legs.

"I really like you, Janelle, which is rare because only one woman has ever had my heart, but it's just something about you that I like. If I find out that you on some slick shit, I'ma kill you and then I might kill your parents, too. You think I won't?" he asked as he looked down at me with sweating rolling down the sides of his face.

"I wouldn't do that. I'm not even friends with Sophie anymore," I said saying whatever that I thought would get me the fuck up out of this hotel room. Floyd looked at the guy holding the shotgun and then he looked at me. .

"Janelle, I don't like to be lied to. The last woman that lied to me is dead in a house in Memphis, Tennessee baby. Do I look like I am somebody you play with?"

I quickly shook my head and he sighed. He untied the belt and I felt urine running down my leg. Shit I wasn't embarrassed at all. I was happy to be alive.

"Pissing on yourself ma is not a good look. Go clean up and come back so we can go for another round," Floyd said as he climbed off of me. I jumped up out of the bed and ran into the bathroom. I closed my eyes and let out a deep breath. Why the fuck didn't I just send his ass on his way when he walked into my shop? The bathroom door opened as I contemplated my next move and Floyd walked in naked. He tossed the condom in the trash and looked at me. I had tears in my eyes as I felt the welts from the belt on my neck. His eyes saddened when he looked at my neck and I knew he was a fucking lunatic.

"Janelle, you said you liked it rough. I didn't mean to hurt you baby," Floyd said and walked over to me. He bent down and cupped my face. I gave him a weak smile and he kissed me. Something that Kasam hadn't done. I grabbed his arms and he kissed me harder. I closed my eyes and continued to cry. My emotions were all over the place. Floyd started kissing me on my neck and then licking and sucking my nipples. I moaned and he picked me up. He walked us into the shower and cut the hot water on.

"If you stick with me then I got you, Janelle. Does Kasam fuck with you like this or do he fuck and leave?" Floyd asked as he stood me upright. I shrugged not even caring how he knew I was fucking with Kasam to begin with and he started to wash me up from head to toe. He turned me around and bent me over. I held on to the towel bar as he slid inside of me. I hadn't had un-protected sex in years. Shit, I was saving my clean pussy for my future husband not this nigga, but he had me all in my feelings.

I started moaning and he started hitting hard from the back. I could feel him cum as his penis jerked inside of me. After sex, we washed off and I followed him back into the room. The man with the shotgun sat in his chair holding my purse. He held up the tracking device and Floyd turned to me before I could say anything he punched me in the mouth. I passed out before I hit the floor.

****

Two days later, I sat outside of Sophie's burned up apartment. Like what the hell happened? I had been so wrapped up in my own shit that I hadn't gotten a chance to even check on her. I called her cell phone and the call went straight to voicemail. Floyd's crazy ass popped up into my head and a cold shiver ran through my body. I pressed the pound sign to leave a message.

"Hey, Sophie, I am really worried about you. Your apartment is burned up and now you're missing. I'm going to the cops if I don't hear from you in 24 hours. I love you please call me back." I ended the call and Kasam called me back before I could put my phone away. I smiled and winced from the pain. My jaw was sore as hell from Floyd punching me.

"Hey, Kasam!"

"Hey, Sophie is good Janelle. She's just been under the weather. Ameer said she will call you when she's feeling better," he said in an irritated tone.

"Um, okay, well, why couldn't she call to tell me that?"

"Because she didn't. Look I just got in town and I'm tired as hell. I'll holler at you later." Kasam ended the call and I closed my eyes. That fucking bitch! I took a chance on setting Floyd up for him and he comes to town without even telling me. He was an ungrateful ass motherfucker. I started my car up and I slowly pulled out of the apartment complex. My phone rang again, but this time it was Floyd. I answered it and put it on speakerphone.

"Hey, what's up?" I asked him still mad as hell at Kasam. Floyd was pissed about the tracking device, but once I convinced him it was a chip to my tablet he let it go. He really was a stupid motherfucker.

"Nothing, I miss you. I haven't had that good-good in two days. Meet me at your spot and we can hit up J. Alexander's," he said sounding happy. I'd heard him on the phone with Tatum, which I later figured out was Ameer's wife. When I woke up from him knocking me out, they were talking like they were in love. I didn't see why he needed me around. I was tired of niggas using me and I wasn't doing shit for Kasam's bitch ass, so operation set up Floyd was over.

"Floyd, I know you fucking with somebody, so stop wasting my time."

"Janelle, I don't have time to waste baby. I like you and I actually do miss you. It's fucked up that a woman as beautiful as you can't accept when a nigga really likes you. Get your sexy ass over to your place, so we can spend some time together." Floyd ended the call and I dropped my phone down into my purse. Maybe he did really like me. Maybe I was meant to fuck with him instead of Kasam.

I didn't know where that would put me and Sophie's friendship, but I would think about all that shit later. I was excited to be fucking with somebody that actually gave a fuck about me for once. I smiled and licked my lips. I would keep fucking him raw and try to get pregnant. With a baby inside of me, Tatum would be a thing of the pass and I would be his woman. Yeah, that sounded like a plan to me. Fuck Kasam and everything he stood for. I guess I would be team Floyd for now.

Chapter Thirteen

Sophie

"Tell me you love me," Ameer said as he laid down beside me. It had been two months since he had been shot and my whole life had changed drastically just like he said it would. The girls and I were now living with Ameer and I had taken on the role of being Ahmad's mother. Ameer's wife refused to sign the divorce papers and honestly I didn't know how to feel about that. Thankfully, she had also left us alone. He said that she just up and disappeared on him. It wasn't hard for me to believe because she seemed like the type.

"Beautiful tell me you love me," Ameer said again and pulled me on top of him. I was wearing a white tank top with black leggings and all the food Ameer had been pumping into me made me gain five pounds that I didn't need, but he seemed to love it. I could see the lust in his eyes when he looked at me. I still hadn't had sex with him because I didn't feel comfortable with him seeing my scars.

I licked my lips and smiled at him. Ameer had been more than good to me and my sisters. They were now at a private school with Ahmad. Ameer and his brothers had been spoiling them like crazy. Drew had a Charger because that was her favorite car and Erin had a little two door BMW. Drew hadn't run away yet and was even doing well in school.

Things had finally turned around for us and it was all because of Ameer. I wanted to be able to make love to him, I was just afraid. Hell, the whole situation had me on edge because it felt like I was dreaming. I felt like our happiness could be snatched away from us at any minute.

"I love you, Ameer. I am in love with you," I said while looking into his sexy eyes. Ameer smiled and his hands went to my hips. He had fully recovered from his gunshot wounds and was even walking without a cane. The bullets went right through and hadn't hit any major arteries.

"How much do you love me ma?"

I leaned down and kissed him gently on the lips. I rubbed his smooth baldhead and looked into his hazel eyes. He was so handsome and all mine. That fact alone had me feeling like I was walking on the clouds.

"I love you with my whole heart, Ameer. How much do you love me?"

Ameer's penis hardened beneath me and he smirked. He pulled my bottom lip into his mouth something that he did every time he kissed me and gently sucked on it. I moaned and grinded on his erection. Ameer's hands went to the top of my leggings and he started to pull them down. My heart started to beat fast and I sat up.

"No, Ameer not yet."

Ameer sighed and I climbed off of him. Ameer got out of the bed and looked at me. He was wearing nothing but his Burberry boxers and his body was looking amazing. Muscles bulged out of his chest and arms while his six-pack sat firmly on his stomach. His body was a work of art. I watched him rub his beard and I could tell he was pissed. He also had a rock hard erection.

"So, what's the deal? Are you a virgin? You gotta disease or some shit because we have been together for a while now and you keep running from me. I need to feel you baby."

I looked around the room and thought about what I would say to him. The truth or a lie? I was scared to tell him the truth because it might make him look at me differently.

"There is something that I have been keeping from you," I said in a low voice.

Ameer's eyes narrowed and he frowned. "What?"

I licked my lips and took a deep breath. I was about to tell him something that I hadn't told anyone not even Janelle. It happened right before my parent's death and I had more things to worry about than justice for me.

"I didn't tell you why my last relationship ended. I found out I was pregnant after only sleeping with my boyfriend a few times. He went crazy talking about how I was trying to force him into marriage and he started hitting me. I blacked out and when I woke up I was in a dirty old room and tied up. I was bleeding so bad that I thought I was going to die Ameer."

"My ex told me that once I had stopped bleeding and he felt the baby was dead that he would take me to the hospital. He kept me in that damn basement for four days without any food. I was soaked in urine and starving. Just when I thought he was going to let me go, he grabbed a knife. He cut two four inch gashes into my inner thighs and said that no man would want me then."

"I thought I was going to die in that place, but after watching me bleed for a couple of hours he dropped me off at a nearby hospital's entrance and pulled off. I told my family that I couldn't remember what happened to me. Since I was over 18, the hospital couldn't give my parents any information on what happened to me without my permission. Marcus is now living in Flint and making a name for himself as an attorney. I try to pretend like it never happened, but every time I get naked I see these scars and they remind me of what he did."

"So, it's not that I don't want to sleep with you, it's just I have these ugly ass scars on my inner thighs and this horrible image in my head of what happened to me and I'm just scared. What he did really messed me up," I confessed and look down at the bed. I was embarrassed as hell and angry all over again at Marcus. Granted, I could have gone after him, but I just wanted to forget it had ever happened and then when I had actually decided to press charges my parents died.

Ameer climbed onto the bed and I laid back. He climbed on top of me and kissed my forehead, my lips, and my tears away. His hazel eyes had darkened to the point that they were almost black. I caressed his cheek in attempt to calm him down.

"I'm okay now, Ameer, I just don't want you to be disgusted with me," I admitted to him.

"Honestly, I don't know what to say. I do know that I love you and I'm so sorry all this fucked up shit happened to you. When I said that you wouldn't need anyone else but me, I meant it. I'm a wash away all of your pain ma and no one is ever going to hurt you again. I want you to get dressed and bring your passport. Daddy's going to make shit right." Ameer gave me a chaste kiss and climbed off of me.

The smile that spread across my face could have been seen a mile away. I quickly got out of the bed. I looked around my massive bedroom that I shared with Ameer and smiled. I had been through so many things, but being with him showed me that even a broken heart could love again and be made whole.

I cleaned up what I didn't want the maid cleaning in my bedroom and I walked into my walk-in closet that was the size of my old apartment. I grabbed my Alexander McQueen overnight bag and began to toss things into it. I had no idea where we were going, so I tried to throw a little of everything in it. I packed Ameer a bag and took a quick shower before heading downstairs.

The home that Ameer moved us into was really built on a compound. There was one way in and one way out. Two hours outside of Detroit, it sat in a city with a population of 2500. Besides the nine bedroom mansion that we lived in Ameer also had three other homes in the compound. One for his mother that was getting out of jail in a week and homes for his brothers to live at if they wanted to.

The compound was heavily guarded and honestly it felt like we were the damn Obama's. It was always guards around and they drove us everywhere, but after while I got used to them and forgot they were even there. Ameer had nice cars and had even bought me this beautiful black Ferrari California because he knew that I loved my dad's Ferrari, but we mainly rode in tinted out SUVS. Ameer had the Cadillac truck and I usually rode in the Suburban.

I found Ameer dressed in a navy suit and talking with someone on his cellphone in the kitchen; his back was to me and I could tell he was upset because of how tense his shoulders were. I took a step towards him and Luke grabbed my arm. I turned to him and smiled. Luke was a sweetheart and had been nothing but nice to us. He and Ameer looked like they were the same age and I could see that they were very close.

"Luke, who is your boy over there talking to?"

Luke smiled.

"No one. I heard you two are about to go on a little weekend getaway."

I nodded too excited to speak and he laughed.

"Well, enjoy yourselves. Ameer's aunt will take good care of the kids and she'll be happy to have some girls to spoil. I know she's always wanted daughters."

I nodded then registered what he had said. I looked up at him and frowned.

"You're not coming with us."

Luke shook his head as Ameer walked over to us.

Ameer wrapped his arms around my waist and kissed the side of my neck.

"Nope, Luke is staying to watch over the girls and Ahmad. Reem is going to roll out with us. Maybe we could make a baby on this trip," Ameer said and laughed. Luke joined in with him and I looked away. We were just getting to know each other and he was still married. We had all the time in the world to make a baby. Like when he was completely legit and divorced. I cleared my throat and I felt Ameer stiffen behind me. He turned me around and I looked up at him.

"Oh, so you don't want to carry my child?" he asked and gave me a once over. I was wearing a black maxi dress with a jean jacket and Salvatore Farragamo flats. I felt under dressed standing next to Ameer. He looked good even on his down days. Ameer's custom made suits would put any nigga to shame. I hadn't even took the time straighten my hair. I touched the end of my curly hair and frowned.

"You look beautiful, so fix your face and stop acting like you don't want to carry a nigga's baby. Now, let's go," Ameer said reading me like a book. Something he did a little too well in my opinion.

Ameer exchanged a few words with Luke and we left.

Ameer and I climbed into the back of a black Suburban. Reem climbed in appearing out of nowhere and the truck pulled off. I tried to call Janelle for the 100th time as we rode to the airport. When her voicemail picked up and said it was full, I tried to call her father. I left him a voicemail and asked him to please return my call. I slipped my phone into my bag and Ameer looked at me.

"Is everything okay baby?"

I shook my head and sighed. Something just didn't feel right. I had never gone this long not talking to Janelle.

"No. Do you know if your brother has talked with my best friend?"

Ameer shook his head.

"No, but shit I haven't even talked to Kasam. He's in Miami and I'm sure she isn't down there with him. He doesn't keep the same woman around for too long."

I nodded and leaned into Ameer's side. His body was so warm and comforting. He kissed me on the top of the head and Reem groaned. Ameer glared at him and then looked back at me.

"I'm sure your girl is doing fine. I don't want anyone knowing where we stay at, but I can have Reem take you to see her when we get back. Maybe y'all can go to Vegas for the weekend. I know you tired of sitting in the house and only going to school."

I smiled and leaned up to kiss him on the lips. He was so thoughtful. Even doing things like paying my tuition just to see me happy.

"That's sounds great. We could use a girl's weekend and Vegas would be fun."

Ameer smiled.

"I told you I got you ma." He kissed me and even with Reem sitting next to us I couldn't stop myself from getting carried away in his kiss.

****

A private jet was how we arrived in Italy. I mean Italy. I had been to Spain and the Caribbean Island, but not Italy. I was speechless because it was so beautiful. We shopped at Chanel, Prada, and Bottega Veneta. Ameer and Reem carried so many bags that people thought we were celebrities. Asking what was our names and trying to take pictures with us. Once we arrived at our hotel, Ameer and Reem left to go have lunch with one of Ameer's business associates and I took a much needed bath.

I ordered room service and set up a candle light dinner in the dining room of our suite. I slipped into a red Agent Provocateur lace body suit and waited for Ameer to come back. The doors to the suite opened as I sipped on my third glass of champagne. My nerves had been all over the place, but I was good and ready to make love to my man now. I mean how could I not show him love? He had gone above and beyond for me and I couldn't wait to show him how appreciative I was of him.

Ameer spotted me and quickly turned around; it was then that I realized Reem must have followed him into our room.

"I'll holla at you later, Reem. Go find you some Italian chick to slide up in nigga," Ameer said. He turned back to me and his facial expression was priceless. I had never felt so sexy in my life. I crossed my legs and my red Giuseppe Zanotti's caught his attention. Ameer loved red and that was why I had picked the color out in the first place.

He licked his lips and smiled at me.

"Do you know how beautiful you look right now?" he asked and started walking towards me.

I sat up straight and opened my legs wide for him. The

body suit was crotch less and I wanted him to see my scars before we got anything started. Ameer stepped in between my legs and dropped down to his knees. He traced both of my scars with the pad of his thumb and then he slowly licked them. I didn't know I was crying until Ameer wiped a tear away. He looked me in the eyes and grabbed my face with both hands.

"It's just us baby and I will never let anyone hurt you ever again. You are so beautiful to me and I can't wait to be inside of you." His words melted into my heart and coated my soul. I loved him with all that I had in me.

I smiled and he started to kiss me. It was passionate, sweet, and wet. His hands fondled my breast and his tongue licked my neck. I moaned and opened my legs wider. I needed him so bad to fill me up. Make me whole.

"Ameer, please," I begged and scooted to the edge of the chair. I needed a release so bad. Ameer looked up at me and he licked his lips. He bit my nipple through the lace bodysuit and started kissing a trail down my stomach. My head fell back when I felt his warm breath hit my sex.

His tongue licked both of my lips and he flicked it at my clitoris. The greatest sensations I had ever felt moved throughout my body. I grabbed his baldhead and grinded on his face. He stuck two of his fingers inside of me and started sucking on my clitoris. The way his fingers curved and dipped in and out of me had me moaning and practically humping his face.

Ameer's free hand found my nipple and he pulled on it. My orgasm shot through me and I moaned loudly. It felt so good I thought I was going to squirt and I had never done nothing like that before. Ameer sat up and licked his lips while looking at me. He took off his suit jacket and then his shirt.

He stood to take off his pants and I grabbed his erection as it poked through the holes in his boxers. It was thick, soft, curved and dripping with pre-cum. I licked it all up before it could fall and he moaned. Ameer grabbed ahold of the table as I sucked on the thick head of his penis. I relaxed my mouth and took him all the way in.

"Shit, Sophie! Suck that shit baby," Ameer said and grabbed my head. He humped my mouth and I was happy that I knew how to deep throat because he wouldn't even let me come up for air. I massaged his balls and started humming. Seconds later his salty cum shot off into my mouth.

I swallowed it all and he stood me up. He bent me over the table and slapped my ass.

"Shit baby that was the best head a nigga ever had," Ameer exclaimed. He dropped down to his knees and I felt him massage my ass. He started to kiss it and then I felt his tongue slide into it. The feeling was incredible. I moaned, bit down onto my bottom lip, and made it shake for him. His finger went back into my sex and he started to pump his tongue and his finger in and out of me. The pressure to come built up inside of me once again.

Ameer smacked my ass really hard and I came all over his finger and the table. I pushed a few candles away from me as Ameer stood. He turned me around and picked me up. I was beyond relieved. My legs were wobbling and I didn't think I could take having sex with him standing up.

He carried me to the bed and took off his boxers. I slipped out of my shoes and my bodysuit. Ameer climbed in between my legs after putting on a condom and looked down at me. I touched his lip with the tip of my finger and he gently bit down on it.

"I love you so much, Ameer," I said while looking up at him. He had me feeling so raw and exposed. I had never been so happy and I needed him to know. He slowly slid into me and I held onto his arms for support. I didn't know if I would be able to take all of him. He was so long and thick. Ameer stopped moving and he kissed me hard. He looked into my eyes and smiled at me.

"Be a big girl and take this dick ma. You had a nigga waiting long enough." With that being said I opened my legs wider and he slipped all the way inside of me. I felt a mixture of pain and pleasure. I closed my eyes and exhaled. Ameer kissed my neck and he started to move. The more he stroked me the wetter I got. I was in a complete state of euphoria.

When Ameer put my legs onto his shoulders, I came with a loud cry and he smiled. I vaguely remember him taking the condom off and flipping me over. I came two more times before he did and I was too tired to say anything other than I love you before falling asleep onto his chest.

Chapter Fourteen

Ameer

"See, what I don't like is for a nigga to hit on a woman. Yes some bitches need a good slapping every now and then, but to beat your baby up out of a woman is just downright fucked up. You had to know that shit was going to come back to haunt you," I said and looked at Sophie's ex. He was tied to a chair and looking at me with nothing but fear in his eyes. I had been back from Italy not even a whole fucking day and all that had been on my mind on the flight home was getting this nigga. I had Luke pick him up and take him to one of my warehouses that I use.

I shook my head at his weak ass and laughed. "Don't

get scared now. You fucking beat a baby that was yours out of my girl and so you gon' to take this ass whooping." I looked at Reem and nodded.

"Untie the nigga." Reem frowned, but did what he was told. Marcus rubbed his wrist after they were free and looked at me. The nigga was clean in a three-piece suit, but he wasn't me. His suit didn't even look custom made. I finished off my blunt and tossed it on the ground.

"Come on nigga I don't have all day. For the shit you did to Sophie I gotta beat that ass."

Marcus slowly stood up and popped his neck. Reem and Aamil started laughing. Luke on the other hand looked at Marcus with nothing but death in his eyes. He cared about Sophie and as I told him about what Marcus did to her all he did was clean his gun. He was ready to murder the nigga and get it over with.

I took off my suit jacket and walked over to Marcus. Marcus tried to hit me in the face and I ducked. I quickly lifted up and punched him in the jaw. He stumbled back and I went in on his ass. I punched him back to back in his face. His nose started leaking and when I heard that crack, I smiled. He fell to the ground and I put my hands on my knees to catch my second wind. I hadn't fought a nigga in years. I shook my head and smiled at him.

"Shit nigga I'm tired. I was going to let you go, but I just can't. You fucked my baby up and for that nigga you going to pay with your life. Luke finish his ass." I stood up and Luke walked over to him. Luke put two bullets into his head as I walked over to Reem and Aamil.

"So does Princeton have the bitch in the other room?" I asked them.

"Yeah, let's go see what she has for us. Floyd hasn't called, so it's not looking too good for her ass," Reem replied. I nodded and Aamil handed me a rag. I wiped my hands clean and we walked out of the room. We went into the room next to it and Princeton stood near the wall with his arms folded across his chest.

A sexy ass looking chick sat in the middle of the floor tied to a chair. She was only wearing her bra and panties and looked like she was pissed the fuck off. I walked over to her and she looked up at me. I loved Sophie, but a nigga wasn't blind. This bitch was fine as hell. Too bad she had fucked with the losing team and now her ass was paying for it.

"Beautiful, I have been on a 10 hour flight. I'm tired

than a motherfucker. So if you could tell me something that could save your life, what would it be?"

She shook her head and looked at Princeton. I could see her trying to plead with him to say something, but the shit wasn't happening. I was tired of Floyd and the nigga was going to come out of hiding one way or another. I'd give him a funeral to go to everyday if I had too. I touched her arm and she jumped.

"Look at me ma. I'm the one calling the shots. Say something bitch and say it quick."

Her eyes narrowed to slits and she chucked up a glob of saliva and spit it in my face. That shit shot in my eye and I saw red. I grabbed her by her hair and slapped the shit out of her. I wiped the spit away with the sleeve of my shirt and slapped her ass again. I was done and I had never felt so disrespected in my life. The bitch wanted to play and I was too tired to join in with her.

"Princeton, take care of her and send her head to his momma's house in Memphis. Y'all have a goodnight, I'm going home to my girl." I walked out of the room as the girl started to scream. The bitch should have talked when she had the chance. As I walked out of the warehouse, I made eye contact with Luke. He was leaning against the truck with a deep frown on his face.

"What's wrong?"

Luke shook his head and opened the truck door. I looked in the back and there was Tatum passed out. She was wearing dirty ass clothes and her face had been badly beaten. The nigga in me was like fuck her, but the husband in me felt bad. I honestly hadn't thought about her in months and here she was looking all fucked up. I touched her bare foot and looked at Luke.

"How did she know we was here?"

Luke looked at Tatum and then my hand on her foot. I could see his disgust with her, but right hand or not no one told me what the fuck to do.

"She didn't. One of my men caught her trying to prostitute by one of the spots. It seems suspect as hell to me," he replied. I nodded because I didn't trust her ass either and looked back at her. Technically, she was still my wife. She was Ahmad's mother and I didn't want her out there like that. I sighed and climbed into the truck. Luke got in the front seat and looked back at me.

"What about, Sophie?" he asked. I gripped Tatum's

foot harder getting a little pissed with Luke because he was really pissing me the fuck off. I wasn't fucking heartless; I couldn't just leave her out on the street.

"Sophie will be fine. Just go to my house in Southfield."

Luke pressed his lips together and turned around. He pulled off and I sat back in my seat. I was so fucking tired and I still couldn't get home to my baby. I needed to set Tatum up, so that she could get her shit together and I needed for her to sign them damn divorce papers. I would holler at Sophie in the morning and let her know I was good. I just wasn't going to be able to rest until all of this shit was out of the way. Aamil kept saying that he was ready to take my place yet his ass hadn't stepped up to do shit. It was time for me to put some fire up under his ass because I was ready to let this part of my life go.

We made it to my house in Southfield around 2:00 in the morning. Luke's men were already outside when we pulled up. I carried Tatum into the first house that we ever lived in together. I took her upstairs straight into the bathroom that was in the master bedroom because she was filthy. I had never seen her so dirty before.

She woke up as I sat her down onto the toilet lid. She

rubbed her eyes and frowned when she saw me. I was dirty as hell, too. I took off my clothes and took her clothes off of her. I sat her in the tub and bagged up our stuff for Luke to toss out before joining her. I sat at the opposite end of the tub and closed my eyes. I felt so relieved to just get a fucking break.

"What are you doing, Ameer?" Tatum asked. Her voice was low and gritty. I shrugged because honestly I didn't know what I was doing and looked at her. Her hair was still dirty and matted down. I pulled her onto my lap and I started to wash her up. When I cut her off, I thought that she would take the money. Her ass had shocked the hell out of me by turning it down.

"So, you tricking now?"

Tatum tried to get off of my lap and I held her down with my arm.

"Are you? Did I not offer to pay you $40,000 a month? What the fuck you doing roaming the streets like a hoe?"

Tatum wiped her tears away and looked at me. In that moment, I didn't think I just reacted. She was looking so fucking beautiful. Her hair was wet and wavy and her face was void of all that bullshit ass makeup. I wrapped my arms around her waist and kissed her neck. Tatum twisted in my lap, so that she was facing me and she slid down onto my dick. I was hard as hell and she was wet and warm.

I tried to pull her up, so that I could get a condom and she started riding the fuck out of me. I grabbed her hips and started pumping into her at a rapid pace. She came and minutes later I came in her. The minute she kissed me on the lips, I knew that I had fucked up. Big time.

I sat Tatum up and I climbed out of the tub. I grabbed a towel and walked into the bedroom. I grabbed my phone and saw that Sophie had called me three times. I shook my head and sat my phone back down. Tatum walked into the bedroom and she looked at me. Her body was still in great shape, but she had lost a lot of weight. I shook my head again as she climbed onto the bed.

"Do I have to get a fucking STD test, Tatum? If I take something back to my girl she's going to fucking kill me."

Tatum laughed and shook her head.

"I'm your wife and you still worried about that side show bob looking bitch. You got me sleeping on the fucking streets just to please her. I fucking hate you, Ameer! I hope and pray you put a baby in me just so I can show that bitch that her pussy ain't golden. You came back just like I knew you would."

I groaned and rubbed my head. It wasn't that Tatum's pussy was better than Sophie's I was just a nigga and a nut was a nut. Sophie's shit was way tighter and she stayed wet like a faucet. Tatum's shit was slowly drying up on her. I looked at Tatum's slick ass smirk she had on her face and got even madder at myself for falling for her slick shit.

"Did you plan this?"

Tatum kicked the covers back and looked at me. The anger she had in her eyes for me matched the anger I had for her. I hated the bitch and I shouldn't have fucked her at all. Raw at that, what the fuck was I thinking?

"You know what, fuck you, Ameer! I was out there because I needed money and I was desperate. I only did hand jobs, but it paid well. I didn't fuck anybody though and that's the truth Ameer."

I laughed and tossed the towel that I was drying off with onto the floor. This shit was getting better and better. I just thought that she was hanging out by the spot to get my attention. I wouldn't have fucked her if I had known she was really tricking. I should have taken her ass to a hotel and left. Now, I'm in some bullshit that could take Sophie away from me.

"If you was jacking niggas off for money then you was sucking dick for money, too. I swear if you burnt me bitch, I'ma kill you." Tatum opened her mouth to reply and I held my hand up and looked at her. "Just go to sleep, we'll talk in the morning about your arrangements and money." She nodded and my phone started ringing again. I cut it off and climbed into bed. Sophie would be pissed, but I knew I could find a way to make it up to her. I'd give her the fucking world if it would keep her in my bed and in my life.

****

I walked into the house two days later. I mean two damn days and with my mother at that. I hadn't called Sophie and I knew she was heated. My closest family and friends were already there waiting for my moms to arrive. Luke had given Sophie specific details on what my mother liked to eat and how to decorate it for her. She had done an excellent job with the place and my mom's favorite flowers; white calla lilies were everywhere. She smiled when she spotted them. I kissed moms on her cheek relieved that she was back where she belonged and ducked off to find my girl.

I found her sitting next to Princeton in the family room.

They were laughing and the shit kind of pissed me off only cause I knew he still checked her out and shit when he thought I wasn't looking. I walked over to them and her whole attitude changed. She stopped smiling and looked up at me.

"You're alive?" she said with a tight smile. Princeton stood up and slowly walked away. I sat in his seat and grabbed her hand. She looked sexy as hell in a black sleeveless jumpsuit with some black pumps. I tugged on her hand and pulled her to my side. I kissed her on the lips and smiled at her. My baby was even sexier when she was mad. I was ready to slide up in my shit.

"I had a lot of business to handle, but I'm good now. I'ma make it up to you as soon as my mom's party is over with."

Sophie pulled her hand away from mines and stood up.

"Gnaw I'm good, do you," she said and walked away. I stared at her ass for a moment and then stood up. I was pissed I couldn't fuck some sense into her because of Tatum's sneaky ass. I couldn't chance giving Sophie anything and I had took a test, but the damn results weren't even back yet. I walked out into the foyer and bumped into Kasam. I hadn't seen his ass in forever. His eyes were glazed over and he looked like he had put on a few pounds. I pulled him in for a hug and patted his back. I let him go and looked at him.

"You good?" I asked. Kasam looked at me and he nodded, but I could see that something was bothering him. I looked at him again wondering what the fuck was his problem this time and out the corner of my eye I saw Sophie walking down the stairs with a small duffle bag. I touched Kasam's arm and shook my head.

"I'll be right back," I said and walked off. I caught up with Sophie as she walked out of the house and over to Luke that was standing by her truck. "What the fuck is going on, Sophie? You leaving me because I was out working?"

Sophie handed Luke her bag and he looked at me. Little did she know, she was getting up out of here unless I said she was. Luke worked for me not her.

"Ameer, I just want to go check on my friend and spend some time with her. Saniyah said she would keep the girls and Ahmad for me. I need a two day break like you," she said with her back to me. I walked up on her and I looked at Luke. He locked up the truck and walked off headed towards the house.

"Sophie, my mom's has been locked up for three years. I know you mad at me, but if you leave without introducing yourself she's going to be pissed. That would be a huge sign of disrespect in her book. I can't have my two favorite girls going at it. I love you girl, stop scaring a nigga and come back in."

Sophie turned around and looked at me. Her eyes were watery and I felt like a piece of shit for hurting her like that. I kissed her gently on the lips and palmed her ass.

"I love you, Sophie. You know that I would never do anything to hurt you baby. I fucked up, but I was out handling business. If I stay out it's so that we can be straight forever ma. You are the only woman that's got my heart."

Sophie stepped back and looked at me.

"Ameer, I don't need this. If you want to do you then just say it. Don't start staying out at night and thinking I'm going to be okay with it because I won't. If the shit happen again you can guarantee that me and the kids will be gone when you get home." I stared at her and I nodded. There was no way in hell I would let her take my son and there was no way I was letting her leave me. I grabbed her hand and pulled her into my arms. She was acting mad, but I could tell she was ready to give in to a nigga.

I kissed her and ran my hands through her straight hair. I slid my hands up her back and kissed her again. I wanted to do all types of shit to her body and I couldn't. That pissed me the fuck off because it was my own damn fault.

"Come on ma and stop tripping. I won't go two days without calling again. I only want you baby and that's the truth. You believe me?" I asked looking her in the eyes. Sophie looked at me and slowly she nodded. I smiled and picked her up. She wrapped her legs around my waist and I stuck my tongue in her mouth. I pressed her against my dick and sucked on her tongue.

"Damn, can you spend a little bit of time with Alana? She has been locked up for three fucking years?" Kasam asked walking up next to us. I slowly lowered Sophie to the ground and she gave Kasam a faint smile. He just glared at her and I pulled her to my side. He was still salty as hell to Sophie for some reason.

"Calm down nigga. Let's go check out momma."

Kasam walked off and Sophie held onto my side tight as hell as we walked away. I needed to see what was wrong with my damn brother. His ass should have been happy as hell to see momma. We walked into the house and I took

Sophie into the formal dining room. My damn phone started ringing and it was like Sophie knew who was calling me before I did.

"You going to answer that?" she asked. I looked at her and then around the room for my mom's. She was sitting next to my cousin Cynthia and they were sipping on some champagne. I took Sophie over to them and my momma looked up at me. Her smile washed off of her face when she looked at Sophie.

"Ma', this is Sophie. Sophie, this is my mother." My mom's lip pressed tightly together as she looked Sophie up and down. My moms was really close with Tatum, so I knew she would be a little pissed about what had gone down between us. Sophie stepped towards her and held out her hand.

"Hi, it's nice to finally meet you," she said and smiled.

"…You too," Moms said dry as hell refusing to shake Sophie's hand. I looked at my moms and shook my head. I really didn't have time for this bullshit. I pulled Sophie to me and kissed her on the lips. She was my girl now and all of them had to accept the shit.

"Ma', I gotta go make some calls. Talk with Sophie and

get to know her. She's family now," I said not leaving any room for argument. I patted Sophie on the ass and walked off.

I called Tatum back and I headed to the basement in my house. Kasam, Aamil, Reem, Bucks, and a few other people were sitting around drinking and smoking.

"Ameer, I want to see momma, I know she's out," Tatum said answering the phone. I sat down next to Reem and stretched out. All the chairs in the front part of my basement were these huge ass suede lazy boy rockers. I had a flat screen that took up the whole wall and a fully stocked bar. A pool table, a round table for gambling, and a kitchen. The other side of the basement was a small bowling alley. I loved my house; it had taken my company two years to build it.

"Sophie…" Shit, my baby was on my mind. "I mean Tatum I'm two hours away from Southfield. I'm not coming back out that way. I'll have her call you later."

"You know what you aint shit, Ameer. You got that bitch at your new house that I haven't even fucking been to with my son acting like she me. Drop off Ahmad and I'll sign those papers. After that nigga you can go to hell for all that I care."

"Are you high, Tatum? You must have gotten ahold to

something bad because you talking real reckless right now. Go to sleep and get some rest. I'll bring Ahmad and my mom's over when I get a chance." I ended the call and saw that everyone was watching me. "What?" I asked frowning. Tatum knew how to fuck up a nigga's mood.

Kasam looked at me and he laughed.

"Nigga, you the only person I know that turns the wife into the side bitch," he said and laughed again. Uncle Hashim walked into the basement and behind him was Mason our fathers connect and best friend. He was family and hell, the reason we were in a position to do what we wanted. I respected him a whole lot more than Uncle Hashim.

I jumped up from my seat and patted uncle Hashim's arm as I walked towards Mason. I gave him a quick hug and looked at him. Mason was tall with a slim build and in his early fifties. He had met my father when they were teenagers. They became friends instantly because my pops used to hang out in front of his dad's deli. They grew close and decided to start selling for his father and as they say, after that the rest was history.

Mason and my pops became the most lucrative drug dealers in Michigan and started expanding. My pops eventually got locked up for assault, but shit didn't change and Mason didn't either. He still came around and we all still worked together. He was the type of man that wanted his whole crew to be living well. A real nigga for real.

"Ameer, how have you been? I saw that beauty upstairs, so I knew life's been treating you really well," Mason said as we both sat down. I smiled as I thought about Sophie.

"Yeah, I've been good. As you see I'm with someone new. Tatum just couldn't get her shit together."

Mason nodded as he looked at me.

"Then you did what you had to do. A family is work, but you shouldn't have to beg someone to love you. She repeatedly fucked up; I'm proud of you. You could have left her a long time ago and you didn't. Have you taken your new woman to see Shadid?"

"No, I haven't gotten a chance to. So much shit has been going on. Now that moms is out things will hopefully get back to normal. This shit is starting to wear me down, Mason," I confessed.

Mason looked at me. "Then maybe you should let it go, Ameer. We have several things you can do other than this. You don't have to handle this side of the business anymore.

You have proven to us and everyone that you can be a successful businessman. We all see how profitable your record company is thanks to Kasam and then theirs your real estate company. It's practically rebuilding downtown Detroit and I'm just so fucking proud of you," Mason said and smiled.

I nodded and peeped uncle Hashim frown real quick before fixing his face. Something was definitely on his mind, but I knew he wouldn't own up to the shit not now anyway with all of us here. He was a fake nigga, so he would only hate and talk his shit behind closed doors.

A nigga like me would tell any fucking body how I felt about them and I definitely wouldn't be breaking bread with niggas I didn't want to fuck with. Something had changed in him and that shit wasn't for the better. He used to be cool as hell, but I was seeing something different now.

Mason turned to Aamil and he smiled. Aamil had always been really close with him. They even vacationed together. Mason had given him this sweet ass limited edition Porsche for his 21st birthday and shit. I couldn't lie, Kasam and me was a little heated about the shit until Mason dropped us off some foreign shit.

"Aamil, how has things been? You haven't come to see

me in months. My mother has been asking about you," Mason said to Aamil.

Aamil rubbed his hand over his beard and sighed.

"Nothing, I've just been busy. Trying to find this bitch made nigga Floyd. We caught up with his right hand man and we been following him for two days now. We sent his moms a birthday gift and the nigga still in hiding. His ass is a punk for real for real," Aamil replied.

"He sounds like it. If someone were to send anything to my mother's house they would be dead by sun down. I checked into him and he's from here, but has been living in Memphis for years. What made him decide to come up here and act stupid?" Mason asked.

"Shit, I wish I knew?" I replied.

Mason laughed and shook his head.

"It sounds like it's time to make a trip to Memphis then. Fuck him and where he makes his money. If he thinks he can fuck up our money, then we'll fuck up his. I'm sending men down there to shut his shit down as we speak. Shadid knows of my plans and he is getting very upset with this situation."

"And when was I going to be notified of this?" Uncle Hashim asked sitting up in his seat. Mason smirked and looked at him. They were always cordial with each other, but I wouldn't necessarily say they were friends.

"Hashim, I didn't know that I needed your permission to do anything. If I were going to notify someone other than Shadid, it would have been Ameer. Let's not get down here and pretend when we all know what this is," Mason replied.

Uncle Hashim's frown deepened and he stood up. His right hand man Albert took a step towards us and Mason's three men walked over to him. I sat back with my brothers not sure what the fuck to do. I loved Mason, but blood was blood and even though my uncle was on that bullshit, I wasn't about to let him get killed. We would all die in this motherfucka tonight.

"Let's just relax and enjoy Alana's welcome home party. Let's not have the cops back in her presence so soon, Hashim. Plus, I wanted to give the queen her gift that I bought," Mason said and stood up. He walked away and his men followed after him. Uncle Hashim looked at me and he shook his head.

"I see were y'all loyalties lie," he said with a disgusted look on his face. He quickly walked away with Albert trailing after him. I looked at Kasam and Aamil.

"What the fuck just happened?"

Kasam laughed and shook his head.

"Nothing other than uncle letting Mason pull that bitch up out of him."

I smiled and we all started laughing. As we walked up the stairs, I could hear my mother laughing. I looked around for Sophie and was about to go upstairs when my mother grabbed my arm. Her whole face was glowing and I knew Mason had gone all out to please her. She was the most spoiled woman I had ever known and she deserved whatever she had plus more. I kissed her cheek and smiled at her.

"What he get you now ma? A plane." I joked.

She giggled and hit my arm.

"Your father has a jet I don't need that. Come look at my gift." She pulled on my arm and took me outside. In front of the house with a pink bow on top of it was a 2014 pearl white Bentley. I smiled and locked eyes with Mason. He was standing next to Aamil and watching my mom's with a smile on his face.

"It looks good ma. I guess we should take back the Jag that we just got you. I mean we're building houses and shit for you, but I see Mason's gift trumps all the work we put in."

My momma laughed and waved her hand in the air. She looked over at Mason and Aamil and stopped smiling. Her eyes watered and she grabbed my hand.

"You good?" I asked her.

My mom's looked up at me and she nodded. She looked back at the car and her happiness was evident on her face again.

"Oh, please, Ameer, I'll keep it all," she said and gave me a fake laugh. I smiled playing along with her and when I looked across at Mason his eyes were fixed on my mom's. He was looking at her with a deep frown and the whole thing made me uneasy. He caught me starting at him and he quickly changed his expression. He held his hand up calling me over and I turned around. I fucked with Mason but if he was up to some slick shit then as the son of Shadid, I had to handle him.

It seemed like every time I thought things were getting better they got worse. Now I had to worry about what the fuck was going on with him and my mom's. That was some shit that I didn't even know how to decipher. My pops would be home in a year and he had no idea what he was coming home to. We was all types of fucked up.

Chapter Fifteen

Sophie

I sipped on a cup of Remy as I listened to Ameer's momma talk about me like I wasn't even in the room.

"Well, Cynthia, tell me how a bitch can move into another woman's house and act like it's her shit? These hoes out are just fucking ruthless. And do you see how in love with her he is? I gotta find my Tate and see what's really going on because this shit just is not right. I'm not going to even to pretend like I like the bitch," she said and shook her head.

I stood up and walked over to her and Cynthia. Alana was not that innocent, sweet mother that Ameer made her out to be. She was rude as hell and acted like she was my age instead of in her fifties. Yes, she looked good for her age, but she needed to calm the fuck down because mother or not I was not about to allow for her to disrespect me.

"Alana, can I talk with you for a moment?" I asked in the nicest tone that I could muster up. Alana looked up at me and she frowned. Kasam walked into the room and my heart beat just a little bit faster. He hated me and I hated him. Now, it was about to be two against one. That nigga was waiting for the day when Ameer put me out. The shit I dealt with to be with the man that I loved was crazy.

"If you want to talk, you come to me correct little girl. I'm Mrs. Alana to you and where in the hell is Tatum? You okay with breaking up families?"

Kasam laughed and I glared at him. He was drunk and high as usual. I expected him to side with her but instead he stood next to me.

"Tatum aint no saint, Alana. Sophie's actually okay once I saw that she wasn't a hoe. I still don't fuck with her like that because she thinks her shit don't stink, but I don't hate her."

Alana looked at me and then Kasam.

"A home wrecker is a whore son. I leave for a few years and you boys lose the good sense I gave you. I'll decide if Sophie isn't a hoe when I want to now both of y'all can get the hell out of my face. Shit, I'm trying to enjoy being free woman go somewhere and sit down with that shit."

I walked away before I slapped the shit out of Ameer's mother and Kasam followed me. I walked into the kitchen and Kasam poured both of us another drink.

"She just don't like new people, Sophie. She'll get to know you and then she'll be good. In her eyes, every woman that we met is out for our money," he said. I nodded and Erin walked in. She was wearing a striped hi low dress and her hair was in a side braid that mom used to do. She looked so beautiful and high. I sat my drink down and grabbed her arm.

"Are you high, Erin?"

Erin giggled and Kasam looked at her. The way his hazel eyes devoured her body had me mad as hell. I pulled Erin to my side and looked at Kasam.

"She's 17 and practically your sister."

Kasam frowned.

"You're married to Ameer? I could have sworn he was married to Tatum?"

Erin stopped smiling and she looked at Kasam.

"Married to her or not he's with my sister. Also, I've been meaning to tell you for a while now just how fucked up your attitude is. Sophie is a good person and she shouldn't have to deal with your shit or that Momma Dee y'all got up in here. We've been through enough shit in our lives and a little bit of peace would be nice."

Kasam put his cup down and walked towards us. He grabbed Erin's hand and looked down at her. Erin had a deep frown on her face and was glaring at him, but even then I could see that she was affected by him.

"Look at you." Kasam looked down at Erin and he licked his lips. *"Shorty looking at a nigga like she want to fuck him up, sexy eyes pinned me down but she wasn't tough enough. Told her a nigga was who he was and she had to suck it up she was the baddest I had seen and I had to scoop her up,*" Kasam rapped to her. Erin rolled her eyes, but her damn grin was big as hell. Erin looked at me and she shrugged.

"I'm good, Sophie and I won't do anything with him because I don't like his want to be pretty rapping ass."

Kasam laughed and put his arm across her shoulder. I watched them as they walked off together and I finished my cup of Remy. I poured myself another one and started to sip it. On one hand, my sisters and I were back to being happy, but at what cost? I had pulled them into a whole new world and this life wasn't nothing to play with. It didn't take me but a nanosecond to realize that Ameer was into some shady shit. Yes, he had his record company amongst other businesses, but I saw that he hustled everyday no matter what. He wasn't standing on no damn corner, but he was into a bunch of shit that I didn't even want to know about.

I finished my third cup of Remy and walked out of the kitchen. My head was starting to spin and I could barely see straight. Drew was God knows where and Erin was probably fucking around with Kasam. He was 8 years older than her and not who I wanted her to end up with. She would be 18 really soon, but I still just wanted more for her. He had groupies and money at his disposal. I knew he would do nothing but break her heart. Not to mention he had slept with Janelle.

I would definitely have to go over some house rules with Ameer because his brothers fucking my sisters was not part of the plan. I slowly walked up the stairs and into my bedroom. Ameer was passed out on the bed with his phone lying next to his head. It started ringing and something in me screamed grab it, so I did. I walked into the bathroom and shut the door.

"Hello," I said in a low voice. I wasn't scared of Ameer or no shit like that I just wanted to at least see what was going on before I got caught.

"Well, well, well. You thought you had it didn't you? It doesn't feel good when the shoe is on the other foot does it bitch?"

I closed my eyes and licked my lips. My mouth was dry as hell and my heart felt like it was literally breaking in half. I didn't want to believe this bitch, but hell he had been doing some shady shit lately. He was telling me one thing, but his actions were showing me another.

"Bitch, if I was in your shoes, I would be mad too," I said to her too caught up in my feelings to come back at her with something real good to say.

Tatum laughed on the other end of the phone.

"Mad isn't the word for what I am, but I'm still his wife and Ahmad's mother. I'm also who he spent the last couple of days with when you was blowing up his phone. Bitch, he was mines first, so he'll always come back to me. I'm coming for my nigga so watch your back." Tatum ended the call and I begin to look through Ameer's phone. Other than Tatum's sex messages that I forwarded to my phone, I didn't really see anything. I came across a few texts from his artist Giselle that looked suspect, but not anything that I could bitch about.

I put his phone onto the sink and I thought about what my next move would be. The nigga had looked me in the eyes and straight lied to me. That had me thinking about if he had been fucking with different women all along. He gave me all of this hope and was doing the same shit Marcus had done. I had my fucking sisters living here with me. I was taking care of his son like he was my own and here he was fucking the same bitch that he claimed hurt him. He'd ended up being just what I thought he would be. No good for me.

I stood up and dropped Ameer's phone right into the toilet before walking out of the bathroom. I packed a small bag and took some money out of the safe that we had in the closet. I sent Erin a text telling her that I needed a break and I asked her to watch Ahmad. Of course Erin texted me back "okay" followed up with a "what that nigga do?" I text her back "nothing" and I walked out of the bedroom.

I couldn't look at Ameer because if I saw his face I would have either slapped the shit out of him or second-guessed leaving the place I now called home. I just needed some time to think about what I would do and sitting up under him wouldn't have helped the situation.

I crept down the stairs looking around for Luke. His ass was always somewhere in the shadows watching me. I saw Princeton walking out of the front door and I ran after him. I grabbed his arm and he looked down at me. I could see that he was faded and I smiled on the inside. I knew he was the only one that would help me sneak out. Ameer's other friends and workers would just turn they back and say they couldn't help me.

"Princeton, can you please help me get out of here? I really need to go check on my best friend."

Princeton looked around and then he looked back at me.

"Sophie, if Ameer finds out that I helped you leave he's going to fuck me up. What happened?"

I shook my head and my eyes watered. I had a right to leave this nigga if I wanted to. I wasn't his damn property; he didn't own me.

"Just help me, Princeton. Ameer doesn't own me."

Princeton looked at me and he sighed.

"No, he doesn't, but you're his woman and we can't do shit for you without his permission. Where are you trying to go?"

I looked around feeling like someone was watching us and I shrugged.

"Anywhere but here!"

Princeton looked down at the ground and I let go of his arm. All of these niggas was some bitches. How could he let a grown ass man tell him what to do?

"Princeton, forget it. I see you need daddy's approval and shit to help me, so just leave. I'll find another way to get up out of here."

Princeton looked at me with his face all turned up and I knew I had him.

"Ameer ain't my fucking daddy, Sophie. Don't say no disrespectful shit like that to me ever again. Now come one before Luke or somebody sees us."

He walked off and I followed after him. We got into his green Range Rover and he sped off. The guard at the gate let us out without a problem and I exhaled. It felt so good to be away from Ameer's lying ass. I gave Princeton directions to Janelle's place and he started driving that way. It took us forever to get to there and when we did, she wasn't even home. I was pissed! I called her father's cell phone and he answered on the first ring.

"Where have you been, Sophie?" he asked sounding really worried. I instantly felt bad because I had quit without a notice and hadn't told him about me and the girls moving with Ameer. I had been so wrapped in my man that I had left everything else fall to the wayside.

"I've been with my boyfriend. I'm so sorry I haven't called you. Have you talked to Janelle? I can't seem to get a hold of her and I really need to talk to her."

"She has a new number. Is everything okay?" he asked. I looked over at Princeton and watched him text on his phone. It was only a matter of time before Ameer woke up and realized I was gone. I needed to be away from Princeton, so that none of this fell back on him.

"Um yeah, can I come over just until I get in touch with Janelle?"

Princeton looked over at me with his brows pulled together and I looked straight ahead.

"Yes, of course come now. Sandra is at a conference in Birmingham, but I'm here. I'll leave the front door unlocked." Johnny ended the call and my cellphone began to ring. Erin's name popped up onto the screen. I answered it hoping everything was okay.

"So, you done with me?" Ameer asked. I could hear the anger in his voice even though he was talking calm to me. He had never hit me or even raised his voice at me, but hearing him so mad had me a little nervous.

"You fucked up and got caught. Don't call me call Tatum." I ended the call and turned my phone off. I looked at Princeton and I could tell he was nervous, too.

"I swear I won't tell him how I got out. Can you take me to my god-father's house?"

Princeton looked straight ahead and sighed. He dropped his cellphone onto his lap and pulled off. I told him the directions to Johnny's house and he headed that way. He looked over at me and shook his head.

"Man, I should have left your ass at the house. The nigga is going to know it was me. Everybody else probably still there drinking and shit. I done fucked up again," he said angrily. I looked out of the window not sure what he meant by again and prayed he drove a little faster. I knew that Ameer wouldn't hurt him because they were like brothers, but he was really whining like a damn child. I was waiting for him to break down crying.

I jumped out of the car before Princeton could park when he pulled up to Johnny's house and I looked at him. He was sweating and I could see that he was really scared of what Ameer would do and say to him.

"I meant what I said. I won't tell him, Princeton. Thank you." I smiled at him and closed the door. He sped off before I could close the door all of the way and I walked up the driveway. I opened the front door and a sense of calm fell over me. I closed it and dropped my bags. Johnny walked towards me with his arms open wide. I ran into them and I started to cry. I just needed to stay away from Ameer.

At least for a few days to get my mind right and I knew Johnny would be cool with that. I would call Janelle and we would link up. After some time had passed, I would be good and things would be clear on what I needed to do and how I should handle the situation I was in. I talked with Johnny for an hour and then I went upstairs to Janell's room to get some much needed rest. The liquor had worn off and I had a small headache.

I woke up in the middle of the night to the bed dipping. My heartbeat quickened as my eyes tried to adjust to the darkness. I cut the lamp on and almost jumped out of my skin. Ameer was sitting at the foot of the bed with his head in his hands. He sighed and sat up. I looked around the room for Luke and Johnny, but it was just Ameer and me.

"You want the truth here it is. Yes, I fucked up, but it wasn't intentional. Tatum showed up to one of my warehouses and was beat up real bad. Luke wanted me to just park her ass somewhere, but I couldn't. She is Ahmad's mother and I did once really love her. So I took her to the first house that I ever owned and I cleaned her up. I put her to bed and I stayed with her for a few days, so that she could get her shit together."

"She is now staying at that house and two people are staying there with her to make sure she gets clean. She's on pills, so the shit shouldn't be hard. I didn't fuck her and that's the truth." Ameer turned around and looked at me. "I can't let you leave me over this bullshit, Sophie. You gotta get some thick skin if you going to be with me and you gotta always put me first. Never trust what a bitch that wants your nigga says to you. Tatum knows that I love you and she will do anything that she can to fuck up what we have. I'm low-key pissed that you even believed her to begin with. Are you finish with me?" he asked. I looked at him and I shrugged. Hell, I was so sure that his ass was on some bullshit when I first left, but now I didn't know. Tatum was obviously pissed at me for being with him and his story sounded legit. I just didn't have time for the games.

"Ameer, I want to be with you but I'm also tired of being hurt. I took a chance on falling in love and I don't want to regret it. To think that you was over there with her while I was worried about you pisses me the fuck off and I don't need for you to waste my time."

Ameer grabbed my hand and pulled me over to him. I climbed into his lap and inhaled his intoxicating scent. I looked at him and he grabbed my face. His hazel eyes softened as he caressed my face and then slid his big hands into my hair. I hadn't seen the Ameer that Drew claimed was a street legend, but I had seen the man that loved his son and that loved me and truthfully I didn't want to lose him.

"Don't fuck around on me, Ameer," I said looking into his eyes.

Ameer nodded and kissed me on the lips. I closed my eyes and he started to kiss my neck. His hands slide down my back and onto my ass. Ameer gripped it and I felt him harden beneath me. "I'm not fucking around on you, Sophie," he whispered as his soft lips kissed on me. "I love you and I'm not letting nothing fuck that up baby," he said and slid my nightgown off of my shoulders. He turned me around and laid me down onto the bed. I looked up at him as he took off his clothes. Ameer's body looked like it had been hand sculpted. It was too perfect. I licked my lips as I watched him slide a condom on. I loved that Ameer used protection with me because I wasn't on birth control and I was not ready to be a mother. We had slipped up a few times, but he always pulled out.

Ameer climbed onto the bed and I opened my legs for him. He smiled as he pulled my underwear off. My nightgown bunched up around my waist as Ameer grabbed my thighs and pulled them to meet his rock hard erection. He slid into me with ease because I was soaking wet for him. He bent his head to kiss me and pulled my tongue into his mouth. I moaned and he pushed my legs back as far as they would go. I swear I could feel him in my stomach he was going so deep. I gripped onto his arms and he looked down at me.

"Tell me what I want to hear," he said speeding up his pace. I moaned and looked up at him.

"I love you Ameer you know that."

Ameer smiled and shook his head. He spread my legs wider and started to fuck me so hard I couldn't think straight.

"Yeah, I do know that. Now, tell me what I need to hear Sophie," he said and pinched my nipples. I came with a load moan and you could hear how wet I was as he slid in and out of me. Ameer pulled out of me long enough to flip me over and grab a handful of my hair. He pulled me up onto my knees and started to fuck me like it was our last. The tears fell because it felt just that good.

"I'm not leaving you, Ameer," I said and held onto the covers for support. Ameer slapped my ass and it stung in the best kind of way.

"I know now tell your nigga what he wants to hear."

I moaned when he pulled my hair hard as hell.

"I want to have your baby!" I yelled and Ameer slid out of me. He slid back in seconds later and I felt him jerking inside of me. His cum slid down the insides of my thighs as he pulled himself out of me. Ameer climbed off the bed and pulled me with him. I slowly stood up because my legs were shaky as hell and Ameer grabbed my bag off of the nearby chair.

"Go take a quick shower, so we can go," he said looking around on the floor. I watched him with a frown on my face. I was ready to go to sleep not take a damn shower and go all the way back to our house. I pouted and Ameer gave me that look. I groaned and walked away with my bag. I took a quick shower and slipped into a pair of Armani exchange velour pants and white tank top. I pulled my hair into a high bun and stepped out of the bathroom. Ameer sat on the bed in a two-piece black suit with a white shirt that was unbuttoned at the collard. He held a Harry Winston bag and was looking at me with a small smile on his face.

"You know a nigga love you right? Shit I went from wanting to get to know you to moving you into my home. What's fucked up is that I'm married and have a kid with someone that I haven't been in love with in a long fucking time. I want to regret meeting, Tatum, but I can't because then I wouldn't have my son, but I do regret marrying her ass. The way you make me feel got me wondering if I was ever in love with her because it never felt like this. What we have is real baby and I don't give a fuck who likes it because our opinions are the only ones that matter. Do you love me?" he asked looking up at me. I nodded with tears in my eyes. I was speechless and didn't know what to say. I couldn't believe this moment was actually happening. Ameer stood and walked over to me. He grabbed a small box out of the bag and placed the bag on the bed. He opened the ring box and his hazel eyes bored into me. I smiled and he kissed me on the lips.

"Of course, I love you, Ameer."

"Do you trust me?"

I nodded and he pulled out the ring it was a princess cut diamond and so beautiful. He slipped it onto my finger and I couldn't believe how heavy it was. I looked down at it and grinned.

"Do you believe me when I say that you are going to be Mrs. Matin?"

How could I get engaged to a man that was already married? I continued to look at the ring as I wondered just how he was going to pull this one off. Ameer must have seen my hesitance because sat the ring box down and he walked over to the chair. He walked back to me holding a stack of papers. I looked at them and then at him.

"She signed them?" I asked with a big smile. Ameer nodded and tossed the papers onto the bed.

"When I said I was going to hold you down I wasn't playing, Sophie. I can't lose you baby. You have to make the happiest man by marrying me girl. I'ma need for you to carry my babies and ride with a nigga. What do you say?" His proposal wasn't traditional, but it was him and I loved it. I smiled and nodded.

"Of course, I'll marry you, Ameer."

Ameer smiled and pulled me into a kiss. I closed my eyes as I felt the happiest I had ever been in my life. We kissed for a few more minutes and started getting my stuff together. We walked to the door and I remembered that I was in Johnny's house. I stopped walking and looked at Ameer.

"What's wrong?" he asked unlocking the bedroom door.

"Where's Johnny?"

Ameer smiled and opened the door.

"Luke tied him up. He's good though I'll let Luke untie him once we're in the car. He has to know that you belong to me, Sophie. I can't think straight without you around ma. Next time some shit goes down, you come to me. Running to him will only get him killed," Ameer said and walked out of the room holding my bag. I sighed and looked down at my ring. I loved Ameer with all that I had but I just didn't know if our kind of love was healthy.

Chapter Sixteen

Tatum

"So, you came back to daddy?" Floyd asked with a smug look on his face. I smiled at him and looked over at Reem. Hell I had no choice. I wished I could have been with Ameer, but that wasn't going to be an option for now. After I talked with his new bitch on the phone, that nigga came by the house and forced me to sign them damn papers. The look he had in his eyes told me he would fuck me up if I didn't. I was fucked up over it because Ameer was the only man I had ever loved and he just kept hurting me. I didn't want to see him die, but I refused to sit back and watch him be happy with somebody else, especially her.

I looked at Reem and I shook my head. He was tied up and bleeding from the two gunshot wounds to his chest. He followed me over here from Floyd's grandmother's house. I didn't want Floyd to get him, but he got himself into this situation. Plus, at the moment, I really didn't give a fuck about Ameer or his niggas. Fuck them all with a hard one!

Floyd's right hand man Cole hit Reem in the back and he spit blood out of his mouth and onto the floor. Floyd laughed as he started to pour gasoline over Reem. I grabbed Floyd's arm and he looked at me.

"What?" he asked with in an irritated tone. Ameer had

thrown me out like yesterday's trash and the fury building inside of me was unhealthy. I was ready to kill his whole damn family. Reem hadn't stepped in and asked Ameer to spare me, so why would I do the same thing for him?

I smiled at Floyd and kissed him on the lips. He was crazy as hell and obsessed with me to the point where it wasn't healthy, but he was the only person besides Nina that I had in my corner.

"Let me light his ass up baby. This nigga was probably laughing when Ameer threw me out onto the street."

Floyd's face relaxed and he handed me a lighter and a piece of paper. I smiled and looked at Reem. He had taken most of his beating like a "g", but I knew this was going to make his sexy ass sing.

"See if you would have talked some sense into your nigga, I could have talked some sense into mine. Rest peacefully in hell motherfucka."

Reem smiled and spit in my face. Floyd punched him in the mouth as I wiped the bloody saliva away. He was a stupid motherfucker. I would have given up my own damn momma to save my life if I had to. I wasn't ready to die, but I guess he was.

I lit the paper and dropped it on top of Reem's head. He started yelling and Floyd laughed. He grabbed my hand and we walked upstairs. Floyd was hiding out right in the middle of the hood and Ameer's bitch ass still couldn't find him. I loved that man with all that I had, but he was not as street smart as he used to be. He became a millionaire and got way too relaxed. Floyd was paid, but he never left the hood even in Memphis; he had a little mansion in the grimiest part of town. That was the difference between him and Ameer. Ameer got that big head and moved to the suburbs when Floyd made his home right in the middle of the hood.

I sat at the dining room table while Floyd leaned against the sink. He was covered in Reem's blood and yet he still looked good. Reem's yells died down and I was happy as hell. Hopefully, his ass had passed out or better he was dead. I never really liked him anyway. At least I was able to fuck Princeton's old fine ass.

"Look, Tatum, I have killed so many people trying to get to this nigga that it's not even funny. I think we need to find another way to get him."

I looked down at my nails that were in a bad need of a fill in and sucked my teeth.

"And what would that be, Fredrick?"

Floyd laughed and shook his head. He hated for me to call him by his government name.

"Bitch, don't call me that shit, but I think we should grab your son and hold him for ransom. We'll only agree to Ameer dropping the money off and of course when he does, it's the end for the so-called king of Detroit. He look like a sucker for your kid, so I'm sure he'll come when he knows we got Ahmad."

I looked at him like he was crazy.

"No, and I haven't seen my son in months, Fredrick. I don't know where he's at," I sadly admitted. Floyd crossed the room quickly and punched me in the face. My nose instantly started bleeding. I held it as I looked up at Floyd. He had never hit me before.

"Bitch, you seem to think I was asking for your permission. We snatching up that little bastard and we're going to finally be able to kill one of the Matin bitches. You kill the head and the fucking body will fall ma."

Floyd started laughing and rubbing his hands together. There was no way in hell I was going to allow him to kidnap my son. Shit, he didn't care if he hit me and he had my name tattooed on his heart. I could only imagine what he would do to Ahmad. I hated Ameer and truthfully I didn't care about Ahmad, but I wasn't going to hand him over to Floyd.

I nodded to make him think I was agreeing to the shit and he smiled at me.

"Bet go cleanup, so we can go find your boy." He kissed my cheek and walked out of the kitchen. I text Nina and put her up to date on Floyd's crazy ass plans. I needed someone to know what was going down just in case I didn't make it out of this situation alive.

Chapter Seventeen

Ameer

"This shit will not be tolerated! This fuck nigga has taken away a nigga that was like my fucking brother! He killed him, but we might as well have pulled the fucking trigger ourselves. Now, I gotta sit down with his momma and explain to her why her son has to have a closed fucking casket funeral. I don't care what y'all niggas gotta do; find this bitch ass nigga. Just find him and bring him to me. Snatch up anybody that is even connected to him. Put them in the warehouse and make they ass talk. There is no coming back to me empty fucking handed. Am I clear?"

I looked around the warehouse at all of the men that worked for me. For my pops and even people that worked under my uncle that was standing next to me nursing a drink. The men nodded and left out of the building. I took another shot of Patron and sat down at the round table.

My fucking friend was gone and I was in Chicago caking it up with Sophie trying to get back on her good side. He was supposed to be with us, but I decided to bring Luke and the kids at the last minute. I knew that Reem's death had nothing to do with Sophie, but if I had been in the streets with him looking for Floyd none of this shit would have happened. I was the one that sent him and Bucks to Floyd's grandmother's house. Now her old ass was missing and Bucks was, too. I could only assume he was dead, too.

My uncle Hashim sat next to me and he shook his head. He was two years younger than my dad, but he hadn't aged well. My cellphone started ringing and I pulled it out of my pocket. I watched Sophie's name slide across the screen and I ended the call. I hadn't been home in a few days and on top of that I had sent my mom to stay there without even telling her. My mom had her on crib right next to ours, but she wanted to stay with us for a few weeks to spend time with the kids.

The warehouse doors opened and Luke walked in with Kasam following behind him. The look on Kasam's face said it all. He was pissed off and drunk as hell. His eyes were bloodshot red and he looked like he hadn't slept in days.

"So y'all niggas put me on rapping duty so that y'all can handle the streets and look what the fuck done happened! Y'all really fucked up this time. Reem was like my big fucking brother!" Kasam yelled.

Aamil jumped out of his chair and looked at Kasam.

"Nigga and you think he wasn't like our brother, too? Get the fuck on with this bullshit Kasam! Go make a fucking mixtape or something nigga."

Kasam glared at Aamil, but he didn't say anything. Aamil sat down and Kasam joined him. Uncle Hashim looked at all of us and he shook his head.

"I don't understand how this nigga is still alive. Your

father won't be pleased and I'm not going to be the one to tell him. Ameer, next week you make that trip and let him know what's up,"

I took a shot and looked around the room. These niggas had me fucked up. I had just saw pops wasn't no way I wasn't making that trip again so soon and bringing back bad news to him fuck that. Pops loved Reem like he was his own son. He was going to be on 100 once he got word of his death.

"Aamil, you go. You haven't been to see him in seven months I counted it up nigga. It's your turn and take somebody with you. I know you think you fucking untouchable, but be smart nigga and stay your ass out of the strip clubs until this shit is settled."

Aamil frowned and shook his head. This nigga wanted to be the boss, but he didn't want to do shit. I had really fucking spoiled these niggas and hadn't even realized the shit until now.

"Fuck that you go. You want to be the boss, so act like it!" I told him.

Kasam groaned and scratched his beard.

"If y'all don't shut the fuck up. I'll go see the nigga. Y'all walking around acting like bosses and shit, y'all still scared of pops. This shit is silly. I called the tour off until we can get the nigga and I don't give a fuck how y'all feel about it. I'm a get with my niggas and we're going to find his ass. Y'all had y'all chance now give me mines." Kasam stood up and walked to the front door. He turned the knob and looked back at us.

"I can't believe y'all let this shit…" Kasam's words were cut off by gunshots. He ran back into the warehouse and pulled his gun out. We all stood up and pulled out our guns. Luke and his men ran out of the doors.

"Man, how do this nigga keep finding us, but y'all can't find him?" Kasam asked shaking his head while breathing hard as hell.

Luke walked back into the warehouse holding Nina by her neck. Aamil looked at me and he started to laugh. What the fuck was the bitch doing shooting at us? How did she even know where we were?

"Man, now y'all got bitches chasing y'all, too? This shit keeps getting better and better," Kasam said as he sat down. My uncle shot me a look of disgust and put his gun away. He walked out of the warehouse with his men following behind him. I pulled a chair to the center of the room and Luke sat

Nina in it. She looked up at me and her heart shaped face was stained with tears.

"What did you do to her?" she asked while Luke tied her up with a cord.

Aamil and Kasam walked over to me and I stood in front of her.

"Who?" Aamil asked.

Nina looked at him and rolled her brown eyes.

"Nigga, was I talking to you?"

One punch to the face made her scream out in pain. Aamil pulled his hand back and punched her again.

"Bitch, don't forget you're the one that's tied up," he said in a calm tone.

"And you fucking shot at me bitch!" Kasam yelled. He grabbed her by her hair and started slapping the shit out of her. After the fifth slap, I grabbed his arm and looked at him.

"Can I ask the bitch a question before y'all start going in on her? Damn!"

Kasam let her hair go and walked away. "I'm out of here I'm going to see my bitch!" He yelled over his shoulder. I nodded and looked down at Nina.

"Nina, what the fuck are you doing here?" I asked her.

"Ameer, she fucked up, but she still loves you. How could you do her like that? I know you know where she's at."

I frowned and looked at Aamil. He shrugged and we looked down at Nina.

"Nina, what the fuck are you talking about?"

Nina licked her dry lips.

"Tatum. She text me a week ago saying that she was with Floyd and that he was forcing her to kidnap your kid. I checked the text a few days later and when I went to call her phone it was cut off. Did you kill her?"

I rubbed my eye and looked around the room for Luke. We made eye contact and he nodded going for his cellphone. My house was on lock down, but I still wanted to make sure that my family was okay. I sighed and dropped down to my knees. This bitch wasn't making any sense to me.

"Nina, I haven't seen Tatum. She signed the divorce papers and I had Luke take her some money. Why would I kill her?"

"Because she's with Floyd and you found out she shot you."

Her words shocked the hell out of me. I had thought Floyd shot me and what the fuck was Tatum doing with him?

"Nina, how do you know Tatum shot me?"

Nina shook her head and she started to cry.

"Because..."

"Because what bitch?" Aamil asked her.

"Because I was the one driving," she confessed with her head down. She looked up at both of us with worried eyes. "I didn't know what she was going to do. I swear!"

Aamil pulled out his gun and licked his lips.

"Bitch it doesn't matter we forgive you."

Before Nina could respond Aamil put two bullets between her eyes. I looked at him and he frowned.

"What?" he asked.

"Nigga I still had questions for her. Like how did Tatum hook up with Floyd? Your trigger happy ass needs to sit down somewhere. If you're going to take my spot nigga you gotta change the way you do things."

Aamil put his gun away and shrugged his shoulders.

"You do things your way and I'll do things my way. I'm about to hit the block," he said and walked off. I watched him exit the warehouse and I sighed. This shit was tiring. I tried to call Tatum's phone and the operator picked up saying the number was disconnected. I called her mother's phone and her voicemail picked up. I put my phone away as Luke walked over to me.

"Sophie's good and the kids are all safe except Drew is missing again. She had Princeton take her to the mall and he said she dipped out on him."

I laughed and shook my head. Drew had started sneaking out of compound in covert ass ways. Jumping in the back of trucks when people were leaving and shit like that. I knew she missed her parents, but the shit she was doing was uncalled for. The minute we found her I was going to put my foot off up in her ass.

"Are your people out looking for her?"

Luke nodded.

"Okay then lets clean this shit up, so that we can go. I need to at least show my face to Sophie and then we'll head back out."

I helped Luke and his men clean up and we left. Sophie was asleep on her side of the bed when I walked into the room. I stripped down and took a hot shower before climbing in behind her. I kissed the side of her neck and she moaned. Sophie was everything that I wanted in a woman and I had to kill Floyd, so that I could relax and give her the life that she deserved.

I really wished Aamil's ass could step up to the plate and take care of this nigga, but he just wasn't focused and I was tired of asking his ass to do shit. I would handle Floyd and deal with Aamil later. I touched Sophie's waist and I slipped my hand in-between her legs. My fingers found her pussy and she slapped my hand away.

"You haven't been home in a week nigga. Don't come in here at 5:00 in the morning trying to get you some. When you proposed, I thought things would be different, Ameer," Sophie said in a low voice.

I licked my lips and put my hand back between her legs. I found her pussy and rubbed the pad of my thumb against her clit.

"And they will be. I have to get this nigga Floyd. You see what happened to Reem. I can't let this nigga walk away, Sophie. Once he's dead, I'm here with you and the kids full time. I'll let Aamil step in my place and he can run shit until pops gets out and decides who's running what. You my fiancé and this my pussy. Stop playing with me ma and give me what I want."

Sophie closed her legs and squeezed my hand with

them. I bit her on the neck and licked it.

"Stop playing bae and give me that sweet pussy. I need it," I whispered in her ear. I pushed her legs apart and pulled her in front of me so that we were in a spooning position. Sophie tooted her ass up ready for me and I slid inside of her. The STD test had come back negative and I was so fucking relieved. I kissed Sophie's back knowing she liked that shit and I started to slowly slide in and out of her. I needed to fuck her good because little did she know I could only stay for a while. I needed to hit the block ASAP. Murdering Floyd had become the only thing a nigga could think about.

Chapter Eighteen

Janelle

"So, after I talked with that bitch Tatum and found out where he was at them two days that I was answering and he didn't pick up, I left. I went to your daddy's house and I chilled out there. Girl, why did I wake up in the middle of the night to Ameer's ass? He fucked the shit out of me and then he proposed. He showed me the divorce papers signed and everything. I'm so happy that bitch is out of our lives," Sophie said on the other end of the phone. I looked around my new bedroom that was in my new home in Memphis and I shook my head. This bitch. She hadn't talked to me in I don't know how long and still all she could talk about was herself. True definition of a selfish bitch.

"I'm really happy for you, Sophie. So where is Tatum at now?" I asked and rubbed my belly. I was only 6 weeks pregnant, so I wasn't showing, but I felt that shit. I had been throwing up every day for weeks.

"I don't know and I don't care. She even signed away her rights to Ahmad. Let that bitch be someone else's problems."

Yeah, like mines.

"Oh, okay well, I miss you and I'm so happy for you," I said with frown on my face. I did miss Sophie, but then I didn't; my emotions were all over the place. She was my best friend and I loved her a lot, but she was also engaged to my baby daddy's enemy. Let's just go back to that. I actually have a baby daddy a bitch was ecstatic. Sophie had given that bitch

Tatum a reason to need my nigga because she didn't have Ameer anymore.

"Thank you and I miss you *little miss I'm going to open a jewelry store in Memphis*. How could you move and not tell me?" Sophie asked.

I lay back on the bed and Floyd walked into the room. I watched him as he took off his clothes and my heart started to beat just a little faster. I was not supposed to talk to Sophie for any reason. I had already fucked up by telling her I was in Memphis. I thought his ass was still in the "D".

"It was so sudden that I didn't have time to think. I just packed my bag and left. Look I have to go and so I'll call you back later," I said quickly and hung up the phone. Floyd grabbed the phone and looked at the screen. He looked up at me and he smiled. His smiles scared me more than anything because I didn't know if I was going to get nice Floyd or the devil himself. I had learned early on that the two lived inside of him, but it was the nice Floyd that had me falling in love with him.

"Didn't I tell you not to talk to her?" I nodded and he grabbed me by my hair. His hand flew back and he slapped me in the face with my phone that was the size of a damn tablet. I started crying as a sharp pain spread throughout my face. Floyd let go off my hair and kissed me on the cheek. His hands went to my stomach and he started rubbing it.

"I'm exhausted, Janelle, and all I want to come home to is some wet pussy and a hot meal. If I catch you talking to that bitch again I'ma make sure you don't have this baby. Do you think I'm playing?"

I shook my head and he smiled. His eyes softened and I looked at his tattoo of Tatum's name. He followed my stare and climbed off of the bed. I watched him walk over to the dresser.

"You must love this bitch. You still wearing her fucking name across your chest and shit. Why am I even here?" I asked getting upset with him.

"Because you are. Don't let Ameer's bitch turn you against me," he said sliding a shirt over his head. Floyd climbed back into the bed and I rolled onto my side. Floyd slid up behind me and wrapped his arm around my waist. "I flew down here to be with you for the weekend and this what I come home to? Why are you worried about Tatum when you living in my damn house and carrying my baby?"

"Because you're carrying her name that's why."

I felt him tense behind me and I thought he might hit me, but he didn't. He sighed and kissed the back of my head.

"I gave you what no nigga would. A title, act appreciative and worry about things like making me happy and decorating my baby's bedroom. Tatum has nothing to do with what we have going on," he said.

I bit down on my bottom lip and the tears rolled down my face and onto the pillow.

"I gave up my life for you Floyd. You deceived me."

Floyd laughed and it sent chills down my spine. I hated and loved him at the same damn time.

"Deceived you? Janelle, be for real. You knew who I was and what I wanted from the jump. I could have killed you, but I didn't. I saw something in you that the other niggas didn't. Let's be real you was a side bitch until I stepped you up. You with the fucking king of the south now mama and once I take down the Matin family I'll be the king of the north, too. Tatum had her chance and she fucked it up. I'm only keeping her around for a purpose. Once I'm through with her, she's dead, so you can stop worrying about a bitch that aint worrying about you. Okay?"

I wiped my tears away and sighed. Floyd was an asshole, but he was also the only man to ever love me. I was carrying his child and hopefully I would be his wife. He had brought me my own shoe boutique to run and everything. No man had ever invested this much into me and his family adored me as well. Sophie was doing her, so I had to look out for myself. I would sneak and call her when I could, but it was time for me to look for a new bff because I would lose her before I lost this nigga.

"Okay," I replied and his hand started rubbing my stomach.

"Good now let's talk about baby names," Floyd said and I smiled. Thinking of my baby always lifted my spirits.

Chapter Nineteen

Sophie

"Drew, please call me back because were worried about you and it's too much shit going on for you to be playing these games. Call me!" I ended the call and looked around the living room. Ahmad and Erin were watching TV while Alana cooked dinner in the kitchen. I couldn't seem to get rid of her ass. I tapped my foot on the floor as I thought about where my sister could have been. With Floyd still after Ameer, I was beyond worried and Ameer was once again gone. That shit had gotten so old.

I stood up and walked out of the living room. I walked down the hall and I could hear Kasam and Alana arguing about something. I crept towards the kitchen and stopped at the entrance. I could hear them, but they couldn't see me.

"Kasam you need counseling," Alana said.

"For what? We both know what the fucking problem is," he replied.

"Watch your mouth, Kasam. It's not healthy for you to hate women so much because of me and I see the way you watch Erin. She's too young baby."

"Look, don't act like you care now. Yea, you fucked me up bad, but I wouldn't hurt Erin plus she'll be 18 in a few months."

"And you think you can trust her? What kind of spell do these women have over y'all?" She asked.

"The same one you have over dad and Mason," Kasam said with an attitude.

"Mommy, mommy!" Ahmad yelled running up to me. I jumped and turned around. I looked down at him and smiled. I was too shocked from what I just heard to even address him calling me mommy. I knew that Kasam and Alana were now behind me and I refused to turn around. I looked up and Ameer bent the corner. He was wearing dark jeans with a tan collar shirt and Gucci loafers. He looked so damn good. I licked my lips and pulled Ahmad to my side. I had grown to love him so much.

"Y'all got a little convention going on out here in the hallway?" Ameer asked walking up on us.

"Yep, we're just one big happy family," Alana said in a cold tone.

Ameer walked up on me and he kissed me while looking into my eyes. The worry on his face made me feel uneasy. Ameer stepped around me to kiss Alana. Kasam stepped around us and walked out of the front door. Seconds later, I watched Erin walk out the front door. I shook my head and turned around. Alana was staring at me with daggers in her eyes. I stepped closer to Ameer and grabbed his hand.

"Ma', what's going on?" Ameer asked.

Alana looked at me and she smiled so hard it stretched her face. I gripped Ameer's hand. This bitch was up to something for sure.

"Nothing, I just wanted Sophie to go with me to the mall. Of course, we would take Luke with us. It's time for us to bond and make this family whole again," she replied.

Ameer smiled and it hurt me to see him so happy because of her lies. I could only imagine what fucked up shit she was planning to do to me.

"I love to hear that, but today isn't a good day. I'ma need you all to stay in the house for just a few more days. I promise everything will be fine by the end of the week. Do you trust me?" Ameer asked and smiled at her. Alana nodded and returned his smile.

"You know I do baby. Well, I'll take Ahmad downstairs and we'll give you two some privacy. Sophie come see me when Ameer leaves baby." Alana grabbed Ahamd's hand and walked off. Ameer led me out of the hallway and up the stairs. We went into our bedroom and I sat on the bed while Ameer made a call. He watched me the entire time he talked on the phone and his hazel eyes were telling me that something was definitely wrong.

I pushed Alana and Kasam's talk to the back of my head as I thought about what Ameer was about to tell me. After fifteen minutes of listening to someone talk on the other end of the phone, he ended the call and joined me on the bed. He grabbed my hand and looked me in the eyes.

"I love you so much, Sophie. I hate that I brought you into my fucked up world when you had your own troubles you were dealing with. I haven't found Drew, but I will. I'm sure she's just acting out. Luke has his men everywhere looking for her. When we get ahold of her, I'm going to send you all to California. I have a lot of property there and it's safe. You can finish up school and the girls can too. Me and Ahmad would miss the fuck out of y'all, but it would be for the best."

I thought about what he was saying and I frowned.

"Ameer, what are you talking about? We're engaged?"

Ameer let go of my hand and rubbed his head.

"I know. I also know that I have brought nothing but drama into your life. I am a selfish nigga and for months I have been putting you through shit and keeping you by my side. I should have left you alone, Sophie, because I am a nigga with the fucking world on his shoulders. I want to go legit, but I don't know if I can. Not now anyway."

I stood up and began to walk back and forth in front of him.

"Yeah, you definitely a selfish nigga. I've already been through the shit and now you send me away? You could have let me go a long time ago, but you didn't. I love you, Ameer, and I'm not going anywhere."

Ameer looked at me and rubbed the bridge of his nose.

"Sophie, this isn't a request. You're going to California even if just for a year. I gotta switch some shit up and get my life together. I want Aamil to step in for me, but he bullshitting, so I gotta handle things for now. You don't need this stress and drama in your life ma. I'll send you away with some money and place money in all of y'all accounts weekly. I love you baby and I'm doing this for us. Make no mistake about it, I'm coming back for you I just need to know that you are happy and living a peaceful life. Right now I can't give you that."

Ameer stood up and walked up to me. He tried to kiss me and I moved my face. The last thing I wanted to do was kiss his ass.

"Where will Ahmad go?" I asked wanting to take him with me.

"With my aunt. Saniyah knows Ahmad and well, I don't want to send him with you and we don't work out. That'll just make it harder for him in the end. I don't want to do this, but I have no choice. I gotta get you out of harm's way baby," he said and I believed him. It didn't make what he was doing any better though. I looked at him and shook my head. My heart hurt so bad that I almost couldn't breathe. I had lost my parents and now I was losing him.

"Well, I hate you, so you can get the fuck out of my face," I said looking him in the eyes. Ameer bit his bottom lip and nodded. He walked out of the bedroom and closed the door behind himself. I took off his ring and threw it at the door. Everybody that I loved left me. If something were to happen to my sisters I didn't know what I would do. The bedroom door opened up and I wiped my face. I was happy to see he had a change of mind. I turned to look at the door and

Alana walked into the room. She closed the door behind herself and locked it.

Chapter Twenty

Ameer

"So, what's the word?" Kasam asked Aamil. Aamil

shrugged and shook his head. He looked just as tired as I felt. This Floyd shit needed to end now. I had just pushed away the damn love of my life to keep her safe and I was all fucked up. I jumped in my car and left without Luke I was so fucking pissed. So here I am now in a house on the Westside with my brothers. Aamil finally put in some fucking work and had caught Floyd's right hand man slipping.

Kasam walked over to Cole and he started punching him in the face. In between telling him that he was going to die worse than Reem did, Kasam also broke the niggas nose. Kasam walked over to his snake pit and opened it up. He grabbed his snake and started petting it. Aamil and I both took a step back. Kasam loved exotic animals, but I didn't fuck with them.

"Nigga you got one minute starting now to tell us everything you know." Kasam said walking over to Cole. He looked at the snake and smiled. The nigga was bleeding to death with a fucking broken nose and he still wasn't giving in. Shit, I was mad I didn't have this nigga on my team.

"I have nothing to say except Floyd is just one man. He has a brother that is even more dangerous than him. Kill him and get ready to bury your whole family."

I looked at my brothers and we all started laughing. This nigga had watched one too many movies.

"Nigga, fuck them and fuck you," Kasam said. He sat the snake on Cole's lap and started cutting his toes and fingers off. The snake slide up Cole's neck and wrapped around it. It started to squeeze and we watched Cole take his last breath.

After cleaning up the basement, my cellphone started to ring. I pulled it out of my jeans and looked at the screen. The call was blocked and I knew exactly who it was.

"What up nigga you tired of hiding?" I asked and everyone in the room looked at me.

"Ameer!" Drew yelled into the phone. My fucking blood ran cold at the sound of fear in her voice. I took a step back and sat down in an aluminum chair.

"Drew, what's wrong?"

"I was chilling at the mall and Floyd took me!" she yelled.

"So, you thought that I was going to run from you. Nigga I'm the king of the south and after you die I'll be the king of the north. You have two hours to get to Tatum's mothers house. I want 30 million in cash and you by yourself. Don't come and I swear I'll put a bullet in this little bitch's head. Time starts now nigga." The line went dead and I still held the phone. How the fuck was I going to tell Sophie that her sister had been kidnapped because of me? Fuck!

"What's wrong?" Luke asked.

"Floyd had Drew call me and he told me to meet him at Tatum's momma's house with 30 million in cash in two hours."

"Fuck!" Luke yelled and ran out of the warehouse with four of his men following behind him.

"We should call Uncle Hashim," Aamil said.

"For what? So he can say I told you so, fuck that. We'll handle this shit ourselves. I'm a fucking kill this nigga when I get my hands on him," I said and looked at Kasam. "Have Rick come and clean this shit up. Don't leave until he's done nigga." Kasam nodded, frowned, and sat down. I knew he wanted to talk shit, but he knew now wasn't the fucking time.

"Is Erin cool?" Kasam asked and we all looked at him. I had never seen my brother care about any female other than the women in our family. Erin was almost legal, but still. Kasam wasn't trying to be faithful and I didn't want him to hurt her. She was my little sis and I wanted nothing but the best for her.

"I only talked to Drew. I'm about to head to the house now and check on them. If you talk to her do not say shit about Drew being kidnapped. Sophie would never forgive me for this shit."

Kasam nodded and sat back in the chair. I left three men back with Kasam. Aamil and I pulled off headed to my house to grab some money and makes sure everyone else was okay.

Chapter Twenty-One

Tatum

Love was a crazy thing. It felt so beautiful when you

gave yourself a way to it, but when it went sour it tore you apart. I never wanted to be in love again. Love forced me to do crazy things. I had kidnapped Sophie's little sister and love was the only thing that had made that possible because the person that helped me only did it for love. Like I said love was a crazy thing.

I looked at Drew as she slept peacefully on the twin bed. She was gagged and tied up because Floyd was being extra fucking paranoid. I wished we could have gotten Princeton's sexy ass, but we couldn't risk it. I knew he was strapped and when I saw the young bitch I didn't have anyone with me.

Now if Floyd was there both of them motherfuckas would have been tied to the bed. I had spotted them holding hands and shit and I couldn't help but to laugh. I wondered if Ameer knew his bitch's sister was smashing the homies. I only fucked Princeton because Hashim had blackmailed me into doing it. He was a sneaky ass nigga, too. I hoped and prayed his ass got a hot one real soon.

"Bitch, you would be okay if your damn sister would have left my nigga alone. Now your ass is tied up and being held for ransom. I really don't care what happens to any of you bitches," I laughed and walked out of the bedroom.

Floyd and his boys were waiting for Ameer at my mother's first home. My mother moved to Tennessee a year ago. Ameer would have known that if he gave a fuck about me. None of that mattered to me anymore though. I hated that nigga with a passion and I couldn't wait for the day that he was dead, which just so happen was going to be today

Floyd wasn't perfect. He had a tendency to slap a bitch out of the blue and even drugged me up a few times, but I knew he loved me. He even made me stop answering Nina's calls, but I knew once it was all said and done, I could sweet talk her into coming back to me. I just needed to handle this shit first.

I was now at one of Floyd's spots and waiting on him to get back. It was only two guys outside of the house, but I felt safe. No one would be looking for us because everyone thought that the kid were at my momma's old house. Dumb niggas. I walked into the kitchen and sat down at the small wood table. I took a shot of Hennessey and smiled. In no time I would be sitting on someone's island 30 million dollars richer. Fuck all the other bullshit. I went to pour another shot of Hennessy and the back door flew open.

Kasam stepped in with Sophie's sister Erin and smiled at me. I jumped up and ran towards the hallway. Someone grabbed me by my hair and snatched me back. I fell to the ground and Erin stood over me.

"How did you find me?" I asked looking up at them. I mean no one should have known where I was.

"Her cellphone you dumb bitch," Erin said and kicked me in the face. I spit a tooth out of my mouth and Kasam pulled me up. Erin pulled her hair into a ponytail and smiled at me.

"Come on bitch. You want to kidnap people and shit. Do something to me," she said and put her fists up. Kasam laughed and leaned against the wall.

"Bae, you gon' fuck this bitch up?" he asked her. Erin looked at me and I kind of got scared. This little bitch looked like she was about to take my fucking head off. She had already kicked my damn front tooth out.

"Kasam, get this bitch and take me to…" Erin popped me in the mouth and started going in on my ass. I fell against the wall and she started banging my head into it. I tried to hit her but her ass was too fast. I could hear Kasam laughing and that shit was really pissing me off. I screamed and grabbed her hair. This bitch head butted me and kneed me in the stomach.

I bent over and she kicked me in the face again. I fell to the ground and she looked at Kasam. She held out her hand and he gave her his gun. My heart started beating fast as hell.

Please! I'm Ahmad's mother!" I yelled. I cried so hard I couldn't see. The gun went off and my leg got hot as hell. She shot me again in the other leg and I started hyperventilating. I couldn't believe this young bitch had actually shot me.

"Alight, Erin, calm down. Shit we can't kill her just yet. Give me the gun," Kasam said to her. I sighed with relief.

"Thank you so much Kasam. I swear I'll leave and y'all will never see me again."

Kasam bent down and he smiled at me.

"Bitch, why would we let you leave? We just getting started," he said.

Erin laughed and the bitch kicked me in the face again. Everything went black.

Chapter Twenty-Two

Ameer

"Uncle Hashim sent over twenty of his men," Aamil said as we pulled up to Tatum's mother's house. I pulled out two guns and put bullets in my Mossberg.

"Oh, and the nigga couldn't bring himself?" I asked. No matter what kind of issues we had that nigga should have been down to ride. We would have been there for him, but it was cool. As long as I had my brothers and Luke a nigga was good.

"You know how he is. Shit he took forever to answer the phone the damn phone," Aamil said. Our family was all types of fucked up. I grabbed the duffle bag, stuck my shotgun in it, and looked at Aamil. He strapped up his vest, threw his shirt over it, and smiled. I was heated that I forgot to grab mine. I nodded and cleared my throat. I was my fucking brother's keepers. I couldn't take them dying. I sure as shit wasn't about to lose them or my fucking family today.

"Be safe nigga. Pops will break out and whoop my ass if you get killed."

Aamil laughed.

"Go nigga!" he yelled with a smile on his face. I exhaled and climbed out of the truck. I scanned the area as I walked onto the porch. The three-bedroom home looked so cozy, but inside I knew trouble was waiting for me.

I kicked the door twice and it swung open. Floyd stood on the other end with a smug ass look on his face. I stepped to the right and Floyd was shot in the chest. He fell back and I dropped the duffle bag. I unzipped the top when a nigga that had to weigh at least 350 pounds tackled me. I tried to sit up and he pressed a desert eagle to my face.

"Make a move bitch nigga and you done for," he said looking down at me. I stared at him itching to grab my gun from the back of my jeans. The big nigga grabbed the bag and looked in it. "Where's the fucking money!" he yelled and pulled the trigger.

The bullet went through my shoulder and all of the air was knocked out of my lungs. Aamil shot the big nigga and he looked down at me. He looked at my arm and he was shot in the chest. He fell to the ground and I was glad he had on that damn vest. Someone stood over me and I looked at his face. A cold shiver went through my body and I knew I was fucked.

.........To Be Continued.